Classic Chinese Fables

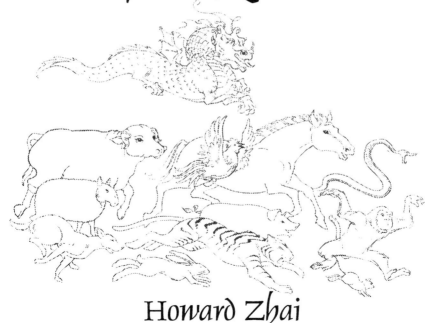

Howard Zhai

101
Classic Chinese
Fables

A Dragon Fly Book
101 Classic Chinese Fables
Published by Dragon Fly Publications Inc.

Translator: Howard Zhai
General Editor: Ruth Martin
Source Editor: Xuejun Wang
Graphic Designer: AccuGraphics Design Inc.
Illustrators: Victor Naval and Bobby Canlas
CD Audio Editor: Ron Rutley

Published in Canada by Dragon Fly Publications Inc.
10371 Mortfield Road, Richmond, BC V7A 2W1
Email: dragon@ihermes.com
Published in the U.S.A. by Dragon Fly Publications Inc.
6233 Potrero Drive, Newark, CA 94560
Email: dragon@ihermes.com

Canadian Cataloguing in Publication Data

Main entry under title:
101 classic Chinese fables

ISBN 0-9682995-0-4

1. Fables, Chinese. 2. Tales--China. I. Zhai, Howard.
II. Martin, Ruth. III. Title: One hundred and one classic Chinese fables.
PN989.C5O63 1998   398.2'0951   C98-911036-2

Introduction

101 Classic Chinese Fables is a collection of fairy tales familiar to Chinese people. Adapted and translated into English, this notable book provides a systematic representation of the genre of the fable in classic Chinese literature. The various fables are grouped thematically into four distinct categories. The format of this book is designed to be enjoyable and practical for reading and teaching purposes.

The original Chinese fables grew out of an oral tradition and were passed down both verbally and in writing forms from generation to generation in China. Scattered in many historical, philosophical, and literary archives, these fables, rooted in Chinese history, date as far back as 1,500 B.C. The early fables began to appear in the works of the Chinese philosophers during the period of Spring and Autumn (770–476 B.C.) and Warring States (475–221 B.C.). The fables at this time, written in the old classic Chinese, are formatted in short stories known as the "Pre-Qin Dynasty Fables." In the Tang (618–907) and Song (960–1279) Dynasties, the genre of the fable developed significantly in the form of the "Story of Wonders," and the "Script for Telling." The classic Chinese fables reached the height of their popularity in the Ming (1368–1644) and Qing (1644–1911) Dynasties. A substantial number of fables were scattered in the works of the "Note Writings," "Speaking Manuscripts," and other types of short stories. The language used in writing fables in the later stage gradually evolved into a mixture of the classic language and the vernacular or "Plain Speaking" language.

The original classic Chinese fables were written and rewritten mainly for the storytelling performers. The wandering storytellers would perform the fables before crowds of listeners. The storytellers acted out the fables with accompanying music either in a public square or door-to-door. They also performed these fables during festivals and celebrations. After their performance, money was usually collected from the audience. Meanwhile, the fables were being taught to children and students in schools.

With the exception of the anonymous authors, prominent philosophers and writers originally created the individual fables selected in this edition. Zhuang Zi (also known as Zhuang Zhou), for instance, is a third century B.C. philosopher and fable writer well-known in Chinese history. Zhuang's story *The Transformed Emperor* has been selected in this translation (see fable 14). Some other celebrated fable writers selected in this edition are: Su Dongpo (Su Shi, 1037–1101, the well-known poet, see fables 23, 26, 67, 82, 84); Liu Zongyuan (773–819, the prose writer, fables 22, 25, 33, 34, 35, 79); Pu Songling (1640–1715, the famous writer of *The Wonder Stories* , also known as *The Ghost Stories,* fable 15). Ai Zi, may be found translated in this edition as *A Prawn for a Dragon Princess* (fable 7) and *The Boasting Magician* (fable 12).

There is a Chinese saying: "The Way has more than one name. There is more than one wise man." This proverb expresses much about the philosophy of the selected stories in this book of classic Chinese fables. They convey a wealth of variants, which aim at preserving the original literary and cultural essence. Some of the themes with which the fables deal include magic, wisdom, and the consequences of sin. The fables employ such literary devices as satire, foreshadowing, metaphor, imagery, and irony. These fables span the spectrum of the classical Chinese literary treasury.

Indeed, the Chinese fables are the Oriental equivalent to the Occidental stories similar to those of Aesop (6th century B.C.), Jean De La Fontaine (1621–1695), and the Brothers Grimm (Jakob, 1785–1863; Wilhelm, 1786–1859). Like this edition of Chinese fables, the Grimm brothers collected fairy tales from around Europe and, selecting the most common formula, originally published them in German. Their collection was subsequently translated into various European languages. Now the collection is available in the most popular languages around the world. The Chinese fables, like their European equivalent, derive from a tradition of teaching a moral lesson to the reader. Some of the fables are humorous, some are sad, others are witty, and others are historical. All aim to teach a strong moral lesson.

This unique collection of classic Chinese fables will delight both adults and children in the English reading world. Told in a wholesome and entertaining manner, the moral lessons are as relevant today as they were in days gone by.

Howard Zhai
Writer and Translator

Ruth Martin
Professor of English

Contents

Introduction

I. Divine and Ghost Fables
1. The Foolish Old Man Who Moved Mountains 3
2. The Great Emperor Who Conquered the Floods . . . 5
3. The Ghost of the Haunted Bridge 6
4. The Bug-eyed Monster of the Haunted Bridge 8
5. The Hairy Monkey Ghost 10
6. Fearless Li Crosses the Graveyard 11
7. A Prawn for a Dragon Princess 12
8. The King God in the Temple 14
9. The Buddhist Monk and the Taoist Priest 16
10. Roast Cow Head 18
11. The Temple of the Mountain Gods 19
12. The Boasting Magician 20
13. The Holy Jade Emperor's Favorite Wine 23
14. The Transformed Emperor 24
15. The Metamorphosis of a Thief 25

II. Animal Fables (Anthropomorphic)
16. The Fate of the Cold Screamer 29
17. The Tale of the Turtle and the Tadpole 30
18. The Screeching Owl and the Wise Turtledove 31
19. The Contentious Bat 32
20. The Leopard and the Dove 33
21. The Drunken Chimpanzees 34
22. The Monkey and the Tiger 36
23. The Clever Ink-fish 37
24. The Donkey and the Tiger 38
25. The Greedy Insect 40
26. The Angry Globefish 41
27. The Poor Night-watch Goose 42
28. The Bird with Nine Heads 44
29. The Myna Bird, the Magpie, and the Dove 45
30. The Fox Who Borrowed Power from the Tiger 46
31. The Animals' Game of Crossing the River 47
32. Mr. Benevolence and the Turtle 49
33. A Fawn's Hard Lesson 51

III. Animal Fables (Non-anthropomorphic)

34. The Hunter Who Blew a Bamboo Whistle. 55
35. Mr. Mouse and Mr. Cat 56
36. The Dim-witted Seahorse. 57
37. The Enraged Bachelor 58
38. The Burdened Rider. 60
39. Tiger the Mouse-cat 61
40. Requesting a Sick Leave for the Donkey 62
41. The Snake's Shadow 63
42. The Turtle Hog. 64
43. How the Brothers' Goose Got Cooked. 65
44. The Greedy Farmer and the Four Fearsome Beasts. 66
45. The Priceless Tiger Fur. 68
46. The Monk and the Pig-farmer. 69
47. The Hunter King 70
48. The Tiger and Tang the Hunter 71
49. The Lost Horse. 73
50. The Scarecrow Fisherman 74
51. The Snake with Legs. 75
52. The Closet Tippler and the Riverside Pigs. 76
53. The Fat Cat 78

IV. Social Fables

54. The Two Braggart Brothers 81
55. Lesson of the Taro Soup. 82
56. The Fragrant Orange 85
57. The Copper Buddha. 88
58. The Careless Thief 90
59. The Monk and the Escort. 91
60. The Magic Mosquito Repellent 93
61. The Burglar and the Fool. 94
62. Like Father, Like Son 95
63. The Digestion of the Pear and the Jujube 96
64. The Boy Learns Several Trades. 97
65. The Rich Man, the Knight, and the Beggar 98
66. Archery Expert Bested by Oil Seller. 100
67. Folk Prescription Liu 102
68. A Calligrapher's Indulgence 104
69. The Swollen-headed Student 105
70. The Quack Surgeon 107
71. The Water Chestnut Tree 108

72. The Sour-tasting Wine 109
73. Pork as Punishment 111
74. The Listening Chess Player. 112
75. Yu Flatters the Emperor 114
76. An Artist Views a Picture 115
77. The Greedy Water. 116
78. The Country of Madmen. 117
79. The Swimmer's Money. 118
80. The Chief Executive Is Besieged. 119
81. The Shadow's Cool Embrace 120
82. The Blind Man and the Sun. 121
83. A Man Gets Flim-flammed 122
84. A Brave Man Learns to Swim. 123
85. The Copper Vase. 124
86. The Blind Man on the Bridge. 126
87. The Discriminating Monk 128
88. The Clean Son-in-law. 130
89. Portrait of an Ugly Man 131
90. The Mistaken Eulogy 132
91. The Light from the Firefly and the Snow. 133
92. A Pot of Boiling Fish 134
93. The Two Stupid Sons 135
94. The Dismantled Bell. 137
95. The Prime Minister's Calligraphy 138
96. The Priceless Zither 139
97. The Rich Monk and the Poor Monk 141
98. The Keen Designer 142
99. The Harmony Brothers 143
100. The Counterfeit Wine. 145
101. Ladies Five, Eight, and Nine. 147

I

Divine and Ghost Fables

I. The Foolish Old Man Who Moved Mountains

Once upon a time, there were two mountains named Taixing and Wangwu, which were situated north of the river and south of the village. These mountains were vast, encompassing an area of approximately one hundred and thirty five square miles and standing about seventy thousand feet high.

A foolish old man who was ninety years old lived in this area. He suffered great inconvenience any time he tried to travel away from his home. One day he summoned his family and asked for ideas about how this situation could be changed.

The foolish old man asked, "I would like to remove those mountains so that they are far away from our home. Does anyone have any suggestions about how this might be done?"

His wife regarded him disdainfully and said, "You are so weak that you cannot move even a small mound of dirt, let alone an entire mountain range. Besides, even if you could move them, where would they go?"

His children all agreed that a great solution would be to throw the mountains into the sea. So the foolish old man, along with all his children, took all of their chisels, picks, pans, and plows, and began throwing rocks and earth into the East Sea. They all worked from early morning to late evening, day after day, relentlessly pursuing their goals of displacing the mountains into the sea.

A teenaged boy from the neighborhood, observing all the commotion, decided to join in the fun. So the entire family of the foolish old man and the teenaged boy from next door worked on and on, not caring if it were too cold in the winter or too hot in the summer; the mountain had to be moved.

A local wise old man finally decided to intervene. Laughing, the wise old man spoke to the foolish old man, "You are making a fool out of yourself and a spectacle of your family. Just look at yourself, so old that you cannot pull a piece of moss off a rock. Why are you trying to move high mountains? You should be enjoying the end of your life doing something fruitful."

The foolish old man replied, "You are both stubborn and complacent. Even my teenaged neighbor friend has a better attitude than you do. Let me explain my strategy. Though I will eventually die, I have many children and grandchildren who will all continue working on this project. As they die off, their children will continue and the legacy will never end. The mountains, by way of contrast, will not grow an inch and can only submit to being cut down. Eventually, I will finish the job that I began through future generations."

As the years passed by and the work of the foolish old man and his children kept going on and on, the wise old man died.

Meanwhile, news of the foolish old man reached the ears of the God Snake in Heaven. Snake decided that he would like to assist the foolish old man with the mountain-moving project. At a meeting in the Holy Palace of Heaven, Snake reported the story to his Holy Majesty, the Jade Emperor God. Jade was deeply moved by the determination, endurance and enthusiasm displayed by the foolish old man and his family. He sent, therefore, two Holy Princes down to earth to assist the foolish old man. The God Princes separated, then moved the two mountains; one was placed east of the area, and the other was placed south. From that time forward, there were no more mountains in the center of the country.

Moral: Heaven helps those who act decisively with enthusiasm, resolution, and endurance.

2. The Great Emperor Who Conquered the Floods

According to legend, in the old days Yu the Great was born as a small dragon from his dead father's tripe. Descending down to earth, he was transformed into the shape of a man. He brought a dragon assistant with him. Yu found the earth covered with water; a terrible flood had devastated the lives of the people. Yu decided to dig great gullies to house all the water. His assistant was ordered to use his great dragon tail to forge huge tracts of valleys throughout the earth. Water from small rivers was guided into big rivers that flowed into the sea.

When Yu turned thirty, he married a local girl. Unfortunately, he ignored his bride and concentrated his attentions on the work of flood control. One day he came to a familiar place and recognized it was his home. He remembered his young bride with fondness and looked forward to seeing her. Before he could see her, however, his work demanded that he leave for another location.

A few years later, Yu again found himself in a place near his home. Instead of going to his house to see his wife, though, he decided that his work was more important and he postponed the reunion. Work began to consume his thoughts day and night and he completely forgot about his wife.

Many years later, Yu's work brought him into the vicinity of his home again. In spite of this opportunity to see his wife, however, he left for more important matters without paying even a glance at her.

After all the years of waiting and longing for her husband, Yu's wife finally turned to stone.

Meanwhile, Yu's years of work had finally paid off and the water overflow was under control; the people were no longer suffering from the flood.

All the people in the land worshipped Yu as a god who had conquered the flood. The Emperor Shun was moved in hearing of Yu's story and abdicated his throne to Yu the Great. Since then, the people cherish the memory of both Yu and Shun as the two Great Emperors in their hearts from generation to generation.

Moral: Greatness requires self-discipline, pain, and sacrifice.

3. The Ghost of the Haunted Bridge

Legend has it that ghosts haunt the Eight Character Bridge in Hangzhou City. Several stories revolve around pedestrian encounters with ghosts on this bridge. A most excellent and favored public bathhouse is housed on the east side of this bridge. In spite of the rumors about ghosts, pedestrians brave the bridge in order to cross to the bathhouse.

One dark, gloomy moonlit night, it began raining heavily. In spite of the dank atmosphere, a man with an umbrella, determined to cross the bridge, plucked up his courage and began walking.

Out of nowhere an apparition loomed before the man and demanded in a shaky, unearthly voice, to share his umbrella. Color drained from the man's face as he acknowledged his first, and hopefully last, encounter with the spirit world. Shaking from head to foot and completely incapable of speech, he managed to side-step the shadowy figure and propel himself forward with the fearful speed of the highly motivated.

The ghost, however, appeared equally determined not to be outpaced. And, with the speed of the supernatural, the ghost seemed to fly alongside the man, repeating its demand to be allowed to share the umbrella.

Now the man's heart was pumping so loudly that he was sure the ghost could hear it. Feeling trapped the man realized that a struggle was inevitable. Could he win against a stronger supernatural force? With nothing left to lose the man stopped in the very middle of the bridge, turned violently towards the shadowy figure and with all his might slammed his body against the terrifying ghost. The ghost was knocked clear over the bridge and into the rushing water below.

Without waiting to see the outcome, the man's legs seemed to take on a will of their own as he bolted off the bridge and over to the safety of the east side.

Arriving in great haste at the public bathhouse, the man's legs gave way. As he lay in the hot comforting water, his trembling stopped and he told the story of his terrifying encounter with the ghost.

After a while another man stumbled into the bathhouse. He was drenched to the bone and trembling violently with fear and babbled almost incoherently about a ghost.

The first man was astonished that the second man had also encountered the evil ghost, and asked him,

"My friend, calm down and explain what happened."

The second man, still trembling with fear, blurted out,

"Don't ask. It was horrible. An evil ghost with an umbrella lured me into the middle of the bridge, then, when I was trapped there, it pushed me into the river. It's a good thing that I know how to swim or the ghost would have killed me for sure."

Moral: Your own superstition could be your greatest enemy.

4. The Bug-eyed Monster of the Haunted Bridge

Located on the east side of the Eight Character Bridge in the city of Hangzhou was a highly favored public bathhouse. In the daytime, people went there to partake of the warm comforting waters. In the evening, many candles could be seen burning in the windows of the bathhouse, a sign welcoming customers to a nice tea service complete with crackers, cakes, and sweets.

One night in late autumn it was raining so heavily that everything was enveloped in darkness. A man was hurrying alone across the Eight Character Bridge searching hopefully for the lighted windows of the bathhouse on the east side. This night he was especially jumpy as he remembered all the ghost stories about this bridge.

Suddenly the man heard footsteps approaching behind him. Fearful that he too might encounter a ghost, he turned swiftly and peered intently into the darkness. Through the gloomy dankness, the man saw an apparition approach: half the size of a normal man, its body shone a slimy brown. It had a huge, bulbous head three times the size of its body.

Horrified, the man realized that this was no ghost. No, indeed. He was viewing a genuine bug-eyed Monster. His face drained of its color and his hair stood up on end. Turning swiftly, he bolted across the remainder of the bridge towards the bathhouse.

As he reached the door, he collapsed gasping for breath. Suddenly the bug-eyed Monster appeared out of the darkness. Now certain that the monster had evil designs upon him, he screamed and threw himself against the door. Falling forwards into the comforting light of the bathhouse, he lay on the floor shaking with fear.

Rolling over from his position on the floor, he just had time to point a shaky finger towards the darkness outside. Suddenly a figure appeared in the doorway. A small boy entered the bathhouse. He was covered with brown slimy mud and wore an adult's bamboo hat; three times his own size.

Comprehension finally setting in, the man asked the boy in a shaky voice,

"Why did you run after me every step of the way to this bathhouse?"

The boy, in an equally shaky voice replied,

"I had just left my grandma's house. She was worried that I would not be able to see in the dark. So she told me to follow an adult."

Moral: Adults should not show superstitious fear in front of a child, otherwise the child will grow up with the same fear.

5. The Hairy Monkey Ghost

Once upon a time, there was a monkey who had ambitions to become human. Unfortunately, he died before his dream could ever be realized.

His ghost traveled to the Nether world where it met the ghost King. The monkey ghost fell at the feet of the ghost King and begged to be allowed to be reincarnated as a human. The ghost King was so moved by the monkey's petition, that he agreed to honor his request,

"I will allow you to become human on one condition. You must first have every hair pulled out from your body."

The monkey ghost was overjoyed to hear what he considered to be an exceedingly reasonable request and agreed to the condition on the spot.

The ghost King summoned the Doctor ghost and ordered him to perform the hair pulling operation on the ghost monkey. As the Doctor ghost extracted some tweezers and began to pull out hair, the monkey could not endure it.

"Stop," cried the ghost monkey. "I've changed my mind. It's simply not worth the pain to become human."

The King ghost laughed and replied,

"Since you have declined to meet the condition you cannot return as a human."

Moral: In order to achieve your goals and objectives, you must be willing to make a sacrifice, and sacrifice involves pain.

6. Fearless Li Crosses the Graveyard

Once upon a time, there was a man by the name of Li the Second. A farm laborer by trade, Li the Second made a living by delivering cotton to the marketplace for his employer.

Li the Second had to wake up in the middle of the night and begin his journey to the market for the morning opening. He regularly traveled with a pole across his shoulders from which hung bundles of cotton on either side.

Each night Li the Second routinely crossed a graveyard. One night he found himself in this wild and desolate place of death and felt the presence of another. The fall wind blew leaves across his feet as he resolutely marched on through the darkness. Suddenly a shadow loomed up from behind a tombstone. Weeping and gnashing its teeth, it began to skip towards Li. In an instant, the apparition was before him. It wore a vivid red tunic draped over a long, flowing white garment, which fell to its feet. Its hair sprang out in all directions and its feral eyes glowed with malevolence. It looked like a female ghost.

Li carefully lowered his pole from his shoulders as the cotton bundles slid off each end. Taking aim, he gave the ghost a good goad, jabbing several clean blows with his pole.

The ghost instantly fell to the ground and gave a decisively human sounding yelp of pain. Now rolling away from the punishing blows, the ghost began begging, again in the most human way possible, for Li to stop jabbing.

Li grabbed the would-be ghost by the scruff of the neck and took a closer look. It was a man dressed up as a female ghost. Shaking the imposter, Li learned that the man frequented the graveyard in order to frighten people. Victims either fainted or were so paralyzed with fear that he could easily rob them of money or merchandise.

Li let fly several more punishing blows before allowing the imposter to promise that he would never pull this stunt again. Eventually the imposter fled in fear for his life. Li calmly placed his cotton bundles on each end of the pole, re-positioned it across his shoulders and continued on his way to the market.

Moral: *Fearlessness is a virtue that serves well when someone tries to take advantage.*

7. A Prawn for a Dragon Princess

Once upon a time, a man named Ai had a bizarre nightmare about a dragon. In his dream, he saw an enormous fire-breathing monster. It wore an Imperial hat on its head and a striking crimson gown on its body. His two round eyes burned with red fire. His mouth, when opened, revealed a seemingly bottomless pit. The monster floated towards Ai's bed and spoke the following words,

"I am the Dragon King of the East Sea. Please do not be afraid of me. I have come to you for assistance. I have heard that you are an intelligent and clever old man who knows many things. It is your wisdom and advice I seek. I have seven daughters. I have found husbands for six of them. The seventh however, appears to be a hopeless case. The problem with her is her temper. Though dragons are ferocious by nature, she is one hundred times worse than any male dragon. If anything at all offends her, be it the slightest thing, or if everything is not done exactly as she wants it, she stirs up wind and rain and pours them down wrathfully on anyone who gives offense. So great is her bad temper that all the male dragons are afraid of her and will not go near her. A dragon husband, therefore, is out of the question. What I want you to do is select an appropriate species of husband for her. He must be gentle and even-tempered, someone who will not react to her rage."

Ai pondered the dilemma carefully. Finally, he replied,

"Majesty Dragon King. Do not worry. I am sure that we will find a suitable candidate. In my opinion, in order for them to be compatible, the husband must be a species from the world of the sea. Now then, let's consider our options.

"Firstly, we have fish. They are very gluttonous. They feed so regularly that they are easily attracted to men's lures and caught. Therefore, fish are not a suitable match for your daughter.

"Secondly, we have turtles. They are not gluttonous and have hands and feet. However, they are extremely ugly in appearance. They are also not a suitable match for your daughter.

"Thirdly, we have prawns. Now the prawn is not gluttonous, it has hands and feet and is good to look at. Additionally, the prawn has an exceedingly good temper. He is also soft, gentle and kind. The most docile creature in the sea world is, in fact, the prawn."

Now the Dragon King wrinkled his brow and pursed his lips,

"But the prawn is a poor and lowly creature, his social status is not worthy of a Dragon Princess."

Ai shook his head in negation and replied,

"Socially, the prawn may not be the best catch for your daughter, but consider his three good qualities: first, he has no belly; second he doesn't bleed after being cut; and third, he reacts to virtually no stimulation at all."

Moral: If you would marry wisely, marry your equal.

8. The King God in the Temple

One day while journeying along the road, a man happened upon a small rural temple. Fields surrounded the area and all was still and quiet. Thinking he would like to enter the temple, the man observed a strange anomaly. A deep moat was trenched around the entire circumference of the temple. And there was no drawbridge that would allow anyone to cross into the temple. The moat was too wide for anyone to jump over. And the muddied waters were deep and full of scum.

The man, however, was determined to take a look inside the temple. Bravely, he hoisted his clothes up high around his waist and began walking through the moat. The filthy waters came up to his chest. Undaunted, he continued until he had safely reached the other side. Once there, he opened the door to the temple and went inside.

Standing in the entrance, he was disappointed by what he saw. Just a stone statue of a once great King. His curiosity sated, he decided to assist the next person who might wish to take a look inside. Dragging the stone statue from the altar, he hauled it across the temple floor. Reaching the door, he heaved the statue forward until it fell bridge-like over the moat. Satisfied with his accomplishment, he then walked boldly over the statue to the other side.

Some time later, a worshipper came to the temple to pay homage to the statue. The worshipper was horrified to see that the great King statue had become a bridge with muddy footprints staining its face and body. Terrified by the sacrilegious treatment of the statue, the worshipper cried out,

"I am so afraid about what will happen because of the blasphemous treatment of the great King statue."

His words were full of reverence and awe as he proceeded to clean the statue with the best silk from his garment.

The worshipper then carefully hauled the great King statue back into the temple and placed it upon the altar where it belonged.

Bowing and kowtowing incessantly before the great King statue, the man slowly backed out of the temple.

After the worshipper departed, the great King statue and a young ghost in the temple had a talk.

Addressing the great King statue, the young ghost said,

"People come from far and wide to pay respect to you. They

bring incense and candles, which they burn, in your honor. They plead with you to spare their lives or the lives of family members. And yet now you have suffered the inexcusable indignity of being thrown down as a bridge walked on and muddied. Are you now going to drop a mighty disaster on the man who did this to you?"

The statue of the great King replied,

"If I did drop a disaster on anyone, it would be on the worshipper who put me back in my proper place."

Now the young ghost was thoroughly perplexed. He said,

"I don't understand. It was the first man who deliberately humiliated you. He is the one who deserves to be punished. The second man respected and worshipped you. Why should he be punished?"

Heaving his stony chest with a deep sigh, the great King statue replied,

"The first man trampled me under foot. Such contempt shows that he has absolutely no fear of me. If he has no fear of me how could I make any trouble for him?"

The young ghost was astonished by this statement, but began to understand something about the abuse of power.

"So," he thought evenly. "This is the philosophy of the statue of the great King: bully the weak and fear the strong."

Moral: Those in power should treat everyone according to their deeds. A true leader is no respecter of persons.

9. The Buddhist Monk and the Taoist Priest

In ancient times, there were two main religious beliefs in China: Buddhism and Taoism. Entire monastic orders worshipped Sakyamuni, their ancestor Buddha. Taoist priests, on the other hand, worshipped their ancestor Lao. In one small temple adherents from both groups would conduct separate worship services. The temple, therefore, housed clay statues of both religions. The Buddhist ancestor Sakyamuni was positioned on the right side and the Taoist ancestor Lao rested on the left side.

One day during the rainy season, a visiting monk entered this unique temple of dual worship. When he saw the positions of the clay statues, he grew indignant.

"It is well known that the left side is a superior position and the right side a subordinate one," he thought. "Why then is our great Buddha ancestor Sakyamuni positioned on the right?"

With firm resolve the monk rolled up his wet sleeves, clasped both clay statues in either hand and switched their positions. Satisfied, he left.

Soon thereafter, a visiting Taoist priest entered the temple. When he saw that the clay statue of the ancestor Lao was positioned on the subordinate side, he grew extremely angry.

"Taoism is the greatest and most honorable religion in the world. Why, then is our ancestor placed on the inferior right side and in subordination to the Buddha?" He thought wrathfully.

Rolling up his wet sleeves, he then switched the two clay statues back into their original positions. He then left as well.

Over the next several weeks, the rain continued to pour. Both the monk and the priest, therefore, had to delay their journeys. Thus, each day they re-entered the temple at separate times. At every new venture therein, each was outraged to see that their clay statue had been switched back to the inferior position. Each immediately put his ancestor back where he wanted it to be. So the clay statues were switched back and forth in the same manner every day, for weeks on end.

Finally, the clay figures became weak with all the wet manhandling. The skin, hair, arms and legs had all re-molded into soggy lumps. The clay remains of ancestor Sakyamuni, with tears in its eyes, said to the clay remains of ancestor Lao,

"My dearest friend, all these years we have remained together side by side in peace. Now we have been damaged beyond recognition by two evil villains."

Moral: *Physically moving someone to a perceived better position is not an act of respect.*

10. Roast Cow Head

In ancient times, there was a man who loved to eat roast cow head. It was his most favorite food. A superstitious person, aware of the man's propensity for cow head meals, warned him:

"If you eat too many cow heads, the spirits of the cows will seek revenge after you die."

The man, not to be dissuaded, ignored the advice and continued to relish his cow head meals.

One night the man dreamt that he had died and that the cow ghosts had dragged him down to the Nether world. When he arrived there, he saw many ghosts who had cow heads or horse heads. As chance would have it, a cow head ghost stopped by his side. Unafraid, the man merely stroked the cow head, then said with excitement in his voice,

"What a nice fat cow head I see. I think that I will roast it and have it for my dinner."

This statement so terribly frightened the ghost that, with the haste of the hunted, it personally escorted the man back to the real world.

Moral: Don't be afraid of ghosts; they are only a figment of your imagination.

II. The Temple of the Mountain Gods

Once upon a time, there was a mountain god temple in the countryside. During the time of sacrifice, the local people would slaughter whole cows to appease the God of the Mountain. The people were warned that if the sacrifices were not made, a great disaster would befall them.

One day, during the time of sacrifice, a traveler arrived from the west; his name was Knowledge. This traveler was appalled with the slaughter of the cows and the people's irrational fear of retribution. The traveler, therefore, boldly entered the temple to have a talk with the statues of the mountain gods.

"Cattle belong to the farmers, not to you. They use the cattle for plowing and working the land. You yourself originated from the earth. The farmers use clay to mold you. Yet you sit here, lazy-like, while they do all the work. Your ego is so great that you even demand to be enshrined and worshipped by these hard-working people."

The traveler then reached for a sharp spear and attacked the statues of the mountain gods. The traveler shattered all but one to pieces.

Exhausted with fighting, the traveler observed the lone statue, that remained. Eventually, the temple monks arrived and grieved over the damage. All the statues, that were destroyed, were gods who ate meat; the one statue, that remained, was a vegetarian. The monks, who were not allowed to eat meat by the religion, implored the traveler to leave this remaining statue intact.

The traveler agreed to leave the vegetarian alone and departed from the temple.

Directly following the destruction of the carnivore statues, the farmers were terrified that imminent retribution would soon follow. They waited in fear.

Days, weeks and months passed and nothing resembling a catastrophe occurred. Eventually the farmers lost all their fear of the mountain gods and stopped sacrificing cattle completely.

Moral: Action stems from either knowledge or superstition.

12. The Boasting Magician

Once upon a time in the State of Zhao, there was a certain alchemist who used magic to deceive people into believing that he was a ghost. He constantly boasted about himself. A certain wise philosopher named Ai saw through these deceptive tricks and resolved to expose the magician for the charlatan that he was.

One day a chance encounter in the capital city Handan provided the philosopher with the means to expose the magician.

Boldly approaching the magician, Ai asked him,

"How old are you sir?"

Winking, the magician said,

"I am unable to tell you my exact age. My earliest memory is of myself and a group of children travelling to visit Fu Xi, the chief of a primitive tribe. Fu Xi was painting a picture: it had eight divine symbols and was in the shape of a man's head with a snake's body. The painting frightened me very much. I spat white foam and fainted into unconsciousness. The old man gave me a special herbal remedy, which cured me.

"My second memory concerns a supernatural incident. This event occurred in the year of Nu Wa. The ancient Emperor burned the stones of five primary colors and used the ashes to mend our sky heaven. The sky sank in the Northwest and the earth fell in the Southeast; I was lucky to be in the middle. Unfortunately, Chi You, the demon King with limitless power, saw me survive and became enraged. He sent his troops to hunt me down and kill me. During the battle, and I am completely truthful here, I pointed my pinky finger towards the demon King and jabbed a hole into his forehead. He fled from me covered with his own blood.

"My third memory involves an encounter with Cang Jie, the great calligrapher who invented the written form of our language. When we first met, he was completely illiterate and begged me to teach him how to read and write. I declined to help him because I thought that he looked like a piece of wood with no brain at all.

"Another memory is of my great friend Yao the Emperor. He threw a huge month-long festival to celebrate the birth of his first son Shun. At his table, I was served a bowl of noodles, fried rice and the most succulent meat I have ever tasted. Years later when Shun was banished from his father's household for making trouble, it was

I who interceded for the boy and convinced his parents to allow him to return home.

"Another time when Yu the Great was struggling with the problem of floods in our country, he wore himself ragged travelling back and forth between disaster locations, not even stopping at his palace for rest or refreshment. Eight times they passed by my home and each time I went outside with rice wine for the Emperor and his escorts; my hospitality alone sustained them through that difficult period.

"I was also friendly with Tang, the Fourth Emperor in our ancestral Dynasty. I remember with fondness Emperor Tang's love of hunting. He had a unique hunting method; he carried a net with a flap in it to catch animals. I teased him often about his habit of eating wild animals.

"At one point, the most skillful fisherman who ever existed lived in the house behind mine. I addressed the lady of the house as 'Auntie Jiang.' And her son was Ziya, the celebrated fisherman. Every time he went fishing at the River Wei, he brought me back a couple of choice fresh fish. They were the best fish I have ever tasted. Even now, I can imagine the succulent fish in my mouth.

"In another year, the Mother Queen of the Heaven Palace invited me personally to the celebration of immortality. I, of course, as the guest of honor, was seated next to the hostess at the banquet table. Unfortunately, I drank too much of the wine of immortality and passed out. Since I was a special favorite of the Buddha, he snapped his fingers and I was immediately transported home.

"At this present moment in time I have an excruciating headache from my hangover, so I have no idea about the day or time."

Ai had had enough. Before the bragging magician could continue with his incessant babbling, the philosopher covered his ears with his hands and hurried away. Ai determined in his mind to wait for a better opportunity to expose the braggart.

A few days later, Zhao the King was in a terrible riding accident. Having been flung from his horse, he suffered from a painful broken rib. The Imperial Doctor informed the King that the blood reserved for a thousand years was required to cure his injury. Everyone in the State searched high and low but the thousand-year-old blood could not be found.

When Ai the philosopher heard about the King's dilemma, he realized that this was a perfect opportunity to unmask the bragging magician. Ai went directly to the Palace where, having obtained an audience with the King, proceeded to outline the magician's remarkable history.

"Your Majesty," concluded Ai, "the magician's blood must be at least a thousand years old, therefore, an excellent cure for you."

The King was overjoyed to hear the philosopher's report and determined to have the magician's blood. A decree for the magician was immediate.

Eventually, the magician was brought before the King. Once the magician heard what the King wanted from him, he began a series of non-stop kowtowing reminiscent of a chicken picking rice from the ground.

"I beg your Majesty not to kill me for my blood. It is actually worthless to you. All those wild stories I told to Ai were fantasies belted out of my big flapping mouth. I have never lived for a thousand years. In fact, just a few days ago, my mother celebrated her sixtieth birthday. My neighbors gave us a lot of wine. I was totally inebriated and told those stories as a joke. Since I know that my good friend Ai loves to hear good jokes, I never intended him to take them seriously."

The magician went on and on until the King had had enough. Now in an exceedingly bad temper, the King had the magician removed from his palace. Additionally, the King made it known far and wide that the magician was a bragging charlatan never to be believed. He was also banned from performing any kind of magic ever again.

Moral: When you make a boast be prepared to face the consequences.

13. The Holy Jade Emperor's Favorite Wine

Once upon a time, there was an enormous celebration in honor of the Holy Jade Emperor's birthday. Supernatural nobles from the Nether world were invited to attend the Imperial party. An edict was issued to serve the nobles from the vat of holy wine. A law from the Nether world stated that a roll must first be taken to ensure that only the nobles received this special holy wine. The supernatural nobles waited their turn in line to officially register their names for the holy wine. An endless line began to circle around the sky; there were just too many nobles waiting to register.

After three thousand years, the roll was still not completed. The Nether world protocol department put pressure on the holy registrar department to speed up the registration, but it seemed to take longer than ever.

Now the Holy Jade Emperor was becoming impatient to have his birthday party. He asked the registrar why the holy wine was not yet being served. The registrar replied, "The supernatural nobles were carried in by their sedan carriers. All the commotion makes registration difficult."

When the Holy Jade Emperor heard that sedan carriers had been flying around the Nether world, he decreed, "If the sedan carriers have been in the Nether world, then they too must be registered."

Seven thousand years passed. Millions of brush pens had been used to write down the names of all the nobles and their sedan carriers. Yet, the job was still not completed.

Now the Holy Jade Emperor grew angry. The holy registrar fell to his knees and pleaded with the Emperor, "Most holy majesty. The delay has been caused because their porters have accompanied the sedan carriers. All those nobles milling around the Nether world have caused a mighty commotion."

The Holy Jade Emperor fell into deep contemplative thought. Finally he shrugged his shoulders and said, "Forget the whole thing. No more registration, and no holy wine for anyone."

Today there are thousands of vats of holy wine still in reserve in the Holy Jade Emperor's wine cellar.

Moral: One must limit the number of guests one invites to a party.

14. The Transformed Emperor

Once upon a time, there were three countries in the primitive world: The South Sea, the North Sea and the Central Land. The Emperor of the South Sea was named "Swifty;" the Emperor of the North Sea was named "Suddenly;" and the Emperor of the Central Land was named "Opaque."

Relationships between the three countries were very good. Always friendly, the three Emperors treated each other with respect.

Now the two Sea Emperors had a solid and substantial appearance. The Central Emperor, however, lacked facial features.

One day Swifty and Suddenly were visiting the Central Land. Opaque received his friends with a warm heart and open arms; his hospitality knew no limits.

Swifty and Suddenly were so overwhelmed with Opaque's hospitality that they wanted to do something to show their gratitude. Swifty said to Suddenly,

"It's a shame that our great friend Opaque lacks a face. Would it not make the most excellent gift if we could give him a face like ours?"

Suddenly agreed that this was, indeed, the very best gift they could give to their faceless friend. Without further discussion, they obtained the tools and set to work.

With chisel in hand they proceeded to give Opaque seven orifices on his face: two for the eyes, two for the ears, two for the nostrils and one for the mouth.

The operation took seven days: one day for each orifice. When the work was completed, Opaque did indeed have a face, however, because he was now a regular man, he became mortal and died.

Moral: Friendship should manifest itself in acceptance.

15. The Metamorphosis of a Thief

Once upon a time, there was a lazy young man who had
never done an honest day's work in his life. He spent his
time wandering from pillar to post. One day he scaled a
wall and stole a duck. Back in his home, he slaughtered the duck
then cooked it and ate it for dinner.

That night while in bed, the young thief suddenly felt itchy all
over. When he awoke the next morning, he was in a sorry state.
Duck feathers grew out from every pore of his body. Not only did
he look absurd, but it was painful too. The feathers felt like thousands of needles growing out of his flesh. He grew very frightened.

The following night he had a dream. He met an old man with
a white beard. The old man informed him,

"You stole a neighbor's duck and ate it. This is why you are
changing into a duck. The painful feathers are the result of your
crime. If you want to return back to your original state, you must
confess your crime to the victim."

When he awoke the young thief could not decide what to do.
Should he go directly to his neighbor and confess or should he wait
for his neighbor to come and confront him with his crime? Since he
was also a coward, he decided to wait.

As he waited, he grew more and more itchy. The feathers were
growing and pushing out like porcupine quills. Finally he could
endure the pain and itch no longer. He went to see his neighbor.

Upon entering the neighbor's home, he was too cowardly to tell
the man the reason for his visit, instead saying,

"Dear friend, I have come to ask if you have lost one of your
ducks? Day before yesterday I saw some rascal darting out from
your front door; he was carrying a white duck under his arm. Now,
I would advise that you do not condemn the thief. It is better to forgive."

The old man smiled and said,

"I agree with you entirely. What is one duck? If the thief needed to steal it then he was obviously hungry. He probably needed it
more than I did."

Now the young thief realized that the old man was kind and
generous. Dropping to his knees, he pleaded,

"I am the thief. I have never regretted anything so much in my
life. I am covered with duck feathers that torment me day and night.

I will never be free from them until you forgive me. Please say you will."

The old man could see the boy's sincerity. He quietly extended a hand towards him and helped him to his feet. Smiling, he said,

"If I don't forgive you, how can I expect to be forgiven for the bad things that I have done? Of course I forgive you."

With these kind words, the duck feathers disappeared from the boy's body.

Moral: A young man can change his bad character by showing courage and telling the truth.

II

Animal Fables

(Anthropomorphic)

16. The Fate of the Cold Screamer

Legend has it that a singularly unique bird lived in the mountain area. She was called the Cold Screamer. The bird had four legs and two large meaty wings.

The appearance of the Cold Screamer changed seasonally. In springtime, the bird developed gloriously soft and full multicolored feathers. She would often be seen strutting around the streams and mountain springs. Constantly preening, she would gaze at her glorious reflection in the water and sing continuously,

"I'm more beautiful than the Phoenix, I'm more beautiful than the Phoenix."

As the seasons changed, however, so did the Cold Screamer. With the autumn winds, she lost most of her glorious plumage. By the time winter set in, the Cold Screamer looked something like a plucked mutated chicken.

Now she could be seen dragging her four ugly feet across the snow, carefully avoiding her reflection in the ice. Her cries were relentless and mournful,

"I'm wasting away, I'm wasting away."

Moral: Our appearance changes with time. We should focus on real character, for all else is vanity.

17. The Tale of the Turtle and the Tadpole

Once upon a time, there was a man named Ai who traveled in his boat along the shores of the East Sea. Mid-point to his destination, a severe storm developed, blowing the small boat this way and that.

Fortunately, Ai was able to maneuver the small craft into a sheltered dock for the night. Eventually the storm died down and all was peacefully quiet.

At midnight, Ai awoke to the sound of a plaintive wailing coming from beneath the water. Astonished and fascinated at the same time, Ai turned his ear towards the calm sea and listened intently. A soft voice arose from beneath him that said,

"Did you hear the news? Yesterday his Majesty the Dragon King decreed that all sea creatures with a tail be put to death. I am a sea turtle, so I have a small tail from birth. How can I try to hide my tail when everyone knows I have one? You on the other hand are a frog and have nothing to worry about. Your behind is smooth and slippery with no tail at all."

Suddenly, Ai heard another unearthly wail emanating from the vicinity near the voice of the turtle.

"Why are you crying?" The turtle asked the frog.

"Because," wailed the frog, "I don't know at what age the Dragon King intends to kill sea creatures with tails. If his Majesty looks back to my childhood, he will recall that I was a tadpole. Then, my tail was longer than any other sea creature. So I might fall under the death penalty as well."

Moral: One must be regarded as he is now not as he was in the past.

18. The Screeching Owl and the Wise Turtledove

O nce upon a time, there was a turtledove resting on a tree. As an old owl friend flew by, the turtledove joined him in flight and asked him a question,

"Where are you going, my friend?"

Completing a graceful arc in the sky, the owl replied,

"The people who live in this area have no appreciation for my singing voice. They shoot arrows and sling shots at me. So I am heading east where I can sing unmolested."

The turtledove, not wishing to lose his friend, exhorted the owl,

"I have heard just the opposite about these people; they love hearing music and the melodious singing of a variety of birds. Perhaps you could adjust your voice so that it is more pleasing to their ears. Furthermore, how do you know that the people back east will appreciate you any more?"

Moral: One should consider every alternative before making a hasty decision.

19. The Contentious Bat

L egend has it that the mythological Phoenix was the King of the birds. On the day that the Phoenix celebrated his birthday every species of bird attended the celebration but one: the bat. The Phoenix did not forget this slight.

One day soon after his birthday the Phoenix noticed the bat flying through the air. The Phoenix ordered that the bat be brought to him. Confronting him directly, he asked,

"Why did you insult me by refusing to attend my birthday party?"

Without hesitation the bat replied smoothly,

"Majesty Phoenix. Unlike you, I also have feet and am able to walk. I am, therefore, not really a bird but an animal classified as a mammal. That is why I did not attend your party—it was for birds only."

Several days later the Giraffe King celebrated his birthday. The Giraffe King was the tallest and largest animal of its kind, so all the other animals showed respect by attending the party. All that is except the bat; his absence did not go unnoticed.

A few days later the Giraffe King ordered the bat to come and see him. Perturbed, the Giraffe King said,

"Every animal which runs on land came to honor me on my birthday except you. Why did you not come?"

Puffing out his chest in an arrogant manner, the bat replied,

"Unlike you, I have wings and can fly. For this reason I am part of the bird kingdom—so I did not have to go to your party."

Some days later the Phoenix King and the Giraffe King met. Eventually they discussed the problem with the bat. They concluded that the bat was a contentious individual. He was, therefore, disowned from both the bird kingdom and the animal kingdom.

Moral: One cannot have a foot in both camps.

20. The Leopard and the Dove

Once upon a time, there was a man named Yie who trained doves to carry messages. He had recently captured a pair of doves that he intended training. He tied up their claws on a perch in his backyard.

Shortly thereafter, a leopard sauntered into the backyard. Observing that the two doves were unable to fly he perceived an opportunity to seize a tasty snack. The leopard leapt forward and plucked the female dove from her perch. As she struggled against the leopard's fierce jaws, the male dove became outraged at this threat to his mate. Ripping his claws from his perch, he swooped down upon the leopard's head and began pecking and biting with all his might.

The leopard was so astonished by this turn of events that he dropped the female dove from his jaws. The female dove, now equally enraged, joined the male in attacking the leopard's head.

With cuts and gashes all around his eyes and head, the leopard made a hasty retreat.

The two doves remained where they were gloating over their victory. The male dove, especially, became puffed up over his win and foolishly lost all fear of the leopard. Now he became bold and reckless, not even bothering to fly to safety when the leopard again approached him.

Suddenly the leopard attacked the male dove again and, without giving him any chance to escape, swallowed him up whole.

Moral: Always be prudent in a battle.

21. The Drunken Chimpanzees

Legend has it that in the region of the Fengxi Mountains in the Sichuan province, there is a colony of unique chimpanzees. These chimps possess the ability to accurately imitate human behavior to the most extraordinary degree. They can both speak and laugh like a man. These chimps are known for imitating a group of men that they saw who got drunk, wore wooden shoes and danced for joy.

Local hunters became curious and decided to test the veracity of the legend. Several pairs of wooden shoes were scattered arbitrarily around the vicinity where the chimps were known to congregate. A large casket of wine was placed in an obvious position on the ground. The hunters then retreated behind the trees to observe the outcome.

Gradually the chimps followed their noses to the casket of wine. The head chimp, perceiving a possible trap, said,

"Don't drink that wine. It's too easy. It can only mean a trap."

All the chimps retreated away from the casket except one. This chimp, having a particular fond remembrance of wine, hesitated. Crouching low, he remained where he was listening and watching carefully for any hint of a trap.

As time wore on and nothing out of the ordinary occurred, the watching chimp began to salivate. He, like the others in his colony, was currently enduring a hot dry season, and was thus particularly thirsty.

Finally, the watching chimp decided that his increasing thirst was worth the risk. Shouting over his shoulder to the other chimps, he said,

"There are no hunters around here. I am parched with thirst and am going to take a drink."

Venturing forward with the boldness of one well aware of all eyes upon him, the chimp then hunkered down before the casket, bent his head down into its contents, and proceeded to indulge himself in a long, satisfying draught.

The other chimps, observing his obvious enjoyment, all darted forward and began helping themselves, one after the other, to the intoxicating beverage.

Soon, the whole colony of chimps was inebriated. Plucking up the wooden shoes that lay around the area, they placed them on their paws and began to dance merrily. Eventually all the drinking and dancing took its toll and every last chimp fell down into a drunken stupor.

Now the hunters seized the opportunity to venture forth from their hiding places and cover the chimps with nets. Now securely bagged and boxed, the hunters carried the chimps off to the city. For years, money was made by all as the chimps performed their drinking and dancing tricks for spectators over and over again.

Moral: Do not attempt to accomplish something that you know is impossible.

22. The Monkey and the Tiger

Once upon a time, there was a special kind of monkey called a Nao monkey. It was very swift at tree climbing and known for its exceedingly sharp claws. High up in the mountain a tiger lived quite near these monkeys. This tiger always had an itchy forehead. Whenever the opportunity presented itself, he would rub his itchy forehead on the trunk of a tree.

One day a cunning Nao monkey observed the tiger's behavior of forehead rubbing. The monkey perceived an opportunity to take advantage of the tiger.

Swinging down from the tree, the monkey sat before the tiger and displayed his long, sharp claws. "If you like," offered the crafty monkey, "I would be happy to scratch your forehead with my claws."

The tiger agreed to try it out and was amazed at how much more satisfying the monkey's scratch was than that of the tree. Thereafter, the monkey accommodated the tiger several times each day by scratching his forehead with his long sharp claws. The tiger enjoyed the sensation so much that he did not notice that the monkey had scratched a hole right into his head. The more the monkey scratched, the more he enjoyed the smell of the tiger's fresh, warm brain. Laughing with joy, the monkey decided to have some tiger brain for dinner.

Digging out a small portion of the tiger's brain, the monkey pretended that it was some bone marrow he had obtained from a southern phoenix.

The tiger trusted the monkey's loyalty so much that he never suspected it was his own brain matter the monkey was chewing on.

Several days and several brain suppers later, the tiger began to feel a pain in his head. Gazing at his reflection in a pool of water, he finally discovered what the crafty monkey had been up to. The tiger, his thinking processes not what they used to be, swung slowly around and sauntered after the monkey in order to exact a just revenge. The monkey, however, quick-witted and well nourished with tiger brain, leapt quickly up into a tree and hid among its sheltering leaves.

With no brain left to speak of, the tiger suffered a terrible headache, curled up his toes, and gave up the ghost.

Moral: Do not accept any offer that will take the advantage from you.

23. The Clever Inkfish

There exists a certain kind of fish called an inkfish. Unique to this fish is a special feature that allows it to spray a black ink-like substance from its mouth. The inkfish does this primarily as a method to protect itself when an enemy attacks.

One day a seagull, while scavenging near shore, noticed a black ball of water. Suspicious of this anomaly, he flew upward and forward for a closer look. The seagull observed that this strange black ball would move from time to time. The seagull determined in his own mind that this strange object must be a type of edible fish.

The seagull dove downwards, scooped up the inkfish and flew away with the prize secure in its bill. The seagull subsequently reported this new and tasty dinner to his fellows.

Moral: Clever people may become victims of their own cleverness.

24. The Donkey and the Tiger

At one time in the province of Guizhou, there were no beasts of burden such as donkeys. The guise people were accustomed to moving everything by themselves.

One day a fearless tiger leapt to the foot of a mountain and observed a donkey playing carelessly. The tiger was both astonished and then afraid.

"My gosh, what is that huge fearsome looking animal," the tiger said. "Maybe it is a supernatural animal sent to the earth by Heaven?"

Not daring to be seen the tiger trembled silently behind a pine bush. Eventually the tiger plucked up enough courage to slowly stretch his neck out from behind his hiding place. Upon closer observation, the tiger perceived that there was nothing unusual or even supernatural about the donkey. This perception puzzled the tiger.

The following day the tiger again hid behind the bush and calmly observed the donkey. Losing some of his fear, the tiger then moved closer to the donkey for a better look. When the donkey finally saw the tiger, he thought the beast was a beaver.

The next day, the tiger became even more bold and moved cautiously towards the donkey. Suddenly the donkey stretched his neck towards the sky and screeched out loudly. This noise so scared the tiger that he lost all his new found courage, turned his tail and fled.

Out of breath, the tiger slowed down and glanced behind his shoulder. Stopping, he noticed that the donkey was not following him. Realizing that the donkey was no threat to him, the tiger returned to the place where the donkey stood.

Emboldened, the tiger tried to tease the donkey. The donkey, however, completely ignored the tiger and continued chewing grass.

The tiger, determined to provoke a reaction, rubbed, scratched, pushed and even nipped the donkey's behind. Finally, the donkey had had enough. Enraged, he jumped as high as he could and bucked his rear legs up high, then fell to the ground. As the tiger stood and observed the donkey's performance, he realized that the beast was not in any way dangerous after all.

The tiger, now secure in his knowledge about the beast of burden, seized the opportunity for a tasty snack. Roaring, the tiger sprang upon the donkey and ate him up. Not only did the tiger overcome his fear, but he also discovered a brand new and delicious dinner.

Moral: Knowledge gives power to the weak mind to take action and gain the upper hand.

25. The Greedy Insect

Once upon a time, in the South there was a small reptile-like insect named Carrier. Carrier was born exceedingly greedy. Anything Carrier saw he reached out and placed upon his back. His back was rough and jagged; hence all objects stuck there quite firmly.

Gradually, more and more objects piled up upon his back making it exceedingly difficult for Carrier to move. One day a man with a kind heart, witnessing Carrier's dilemma, assisted him in carefully removing all the encumbering objects from his back. For the first time in years, Carrier was free.

Unfortunately, as time went on, Carrier fell back into his old greedy ways and again accumulated a heavy load of desired objects upon his back.

One day Carrier, crawling up too high to retrieve yet another desired object, fell over backwards and was crushed to death by the heavy load.

Moral: A greedy heart may be crushed by its own acquisitions.

26. The Angry Globefish

A certain kind of fish exists called a globefish; this fish is goaded to wrathful anger at the slightest provocation. It is impervious to reason and entirely capricious.

One day one such globefish was frolicking in a river under a bridge. Flipping over a bit too suddenly, the globefish bumped his head on the overhanging pier. Furious, the globefish spewed out a series of profanities and curses upon the wooden pier.

His eyes widened wrathfully as he expanded his gills to their fullest. He thus swam in this inflated condition beneath the pier. All the other fish swam around the globefish trying to calm him down. They patiently exhorted him to logically consider the irrational nature of anger focused against a wooden pier.

The globefish, however, did not want to listen to the voice of reason, choosing instead to indulge himself in reckless anger. His already expanded body continued to puff up, as he became even more stubborn and militant with wrath.

His fins puffed out until they became so sharp that his body floated to the surface of the water. At that moment a shark, perceiving a tasty looking snack, swam over and easily swallowed up the inflated globefish.

Moral: Destruction comes upon someone who is easily angered and impervious to reason.

27. The Poor Night-watch Goose

Geese always fly south for the winter. As the wild geese prepare for their winter migration they may be found perching around lakes and marshes. They congregate around one area in particular: the shoreline of Tai Lake. At dusk, the geese settle down in these marshy waters for the night. In order to protect themselves from hunters, the geese always appoint one goose to keep watch. One night someone in the group was appointed as the night-watch goose to watch the flock.

Hunters living near Tai Lake knew that the geese had a habit of appointing a night-watch goose, so they were crafty in their approach. Late that night these hunters lit their torches and crept silently towards the flock of sleeping geese.

The night-watch goose saw tiny flashes of light blinking from behind the rushes, so she quacked loudly and flapped her wings.

When the hunters heard the quacking they blew out their torches and crouched down silently.

Meanwhile, at the sound of the alarm, the other geese leapt up and prepared to take immediate flight. Searching around in all directions the geese observed only darkness and heard nothing. Perturbed by the false alarm, the geese glanced at their night-watch goose disdainfully then went back to sleep.

When all was quiet again, the hunters stood up and re-lit their torches, then stealthily crept towards the sleeping geese.

When the night-watch goose again saw the flickering lights, she quacked loudly and flapped her wings furiously, rousing the other geese from their slumber.

Again the hunters extinguished their torches and knelt down beneath the rushes. And again the geese, on full alert, listened and looked carefully, but all was dark and silent. Again the night-watch goose was in the doghouse, so to speak, and again the geese settled down into a deep sleep.

This pattern repeated itself four times. Finally, the other geese were so upset with the night-watch goose at what they believed to be false alarms, that they attacked her. She was bitten, bullied, and harassed until she fell into a mournful silence.

When all was quiet, the hunters again re-lit their torches and crept towards the sleeping geese. The night-watch goose was so upset by the way she had been treated by the other geese, that she silently flew away.

From her place of safety, the night-watch goose watched as the hunters threw their nets over the sleeping geese and captured every last one of them.

Moral: If you appoint someone to do a job, trust them to do it.

28. The Bird with Nine Heads

Once upon a time, there was a bird who had nine heads. One head would capture the food and the other eight heads would fight over it.

The other birds always knew when the Nine-headed bird was having a meal. It sounded like an entire flock as it cascaded through the trees in a flurry of competition. Every meal was the same, wounded, the bird emerged from the ordeal with all nine heads bruised and bleeding. As it grew older, the constant battles and lack of food made it weaker.

One lone duck, witnessing this situation, confronted the nine-headed bird,

"Just look at yourself. Nine hungry mouths struggling for one piece of food—it is ridiculous. If you keep this up there won't be enough food to feed your one belly. Now listen to my suggestion. Let each head hunt separately for food. That way all nine heads will swallow its own food and there will be more than enough to fill the communal stomach."

None of the nine heads could come to a unanimous agreement. Some thought separate hunting was a good idea, others wanted things to continue as they had always been. No compromise was reached.

In the end the nine-headed bird died from hunger.

Moral: A house divided cannot stand.

29. The Myna Bird, the Magpie, and the Dove

Once upon a time, there were many girl birds who lived together on the girl's mountain. Each bird had her own nest in her own tree.

One day a fierce and hungry tiger leapt out from behind a boulder and threateningly menaced a magpie in her tree.

The magpie, viewing the terrible sight of the tiger, began chirping a song of terror.

The myna bird, hearing the song of the magpie, imitated it exactly. Her song attracted the other myna birds who flew over to the area to join in the fun. Soon the tree was filled with myna birds.

A dove who was flying by witnessed this scene. She found it very strange that all these myna birds were gathered together in a magpie tree singing a song of terror.

The dove perched next to the magpie and asked her,

"Dear sister bird, the tiger's power is limited to the land. Why are you so afraid of him?"

"Sister dove," she replied, "When the tiger roars he blows up a dangerous storm. The force from the wind could blow my nest apart. I am singing loudly to make him go away."

Nodding with understanding, the dove then turned to a myna bird and asked,

"This is the magpie's nest. Why are you here?"

The myna bird seemed confused by the question. After some consideration, she shrugged her shoulders and replied,

"I really don't know why I'm here. All I know is that we myna birds follow the magpies. When one magpie cries, we all imitate it."

Moral: Fools blindly follow the leader.

30. The Fox Who Borrowed Power from the Tiger

Once upon a time, there was a tiger who roamed freely throughout the forest. Every animal in the kingdom was terrified in case the fearsome tiger should venture into view. The one exception was the small fox. Fearless, the fox would boldly approach the tiger and begin a conversation.

"You dare not eat me. I am an ambassador from the Imperial God in Heaven. I have been appointed to represent his majesty as the king of all beasts. If you try to eat me, you will be in big trouble with the Imperial God in Heaven. As proof of my superiority, I challenge you to follow along behind me in the forest and observe how all the other animals clear the way for me."

So they wandered through the forest, the fox first, with the tiger following closely behind. Sure enough, all the other animals immediately scattered in fear before the fox. Seeing how the animals scurried away from the fox, the tiger convinced himself that the fox was, indeed, an ambassador from Heaven. He never did learn that the animals were scattering before the fox because they saw the tiger behind him.

Moral: Do not allow someone to use your name for his own sake.

31. The Animals' Game of Crossing the River

Once upon a time, the Jade Emperor God hosted a party in honor of his Majesty's birthday. His Holy Majesty summoned all the animals to participate in the game of crossing the river. The first twelve species of animals to successfully cross the river would be rewarded by becoming symbols for the year of man's birth as it coincided with the lunar zodiac calendar.

In the wee hours on the morning of his Majesty's birthday when the cock had not yet crowed, the ox called the mouse and the cat to wake up early and get a head start in the contest. At that time the cat and mouse were the very best friends, they lived together like members of one big, happy family. The cat and mouse responded to the ox's call and jumped up happily upon his massive back. They then strode down to the river where all the other animals were supposed to meet for the contest.

When the three arrived in the middle of the river, the mouse began to conceive a plot. Greedy and avaricious, the mouse thought that he alone wanted to win the race and receive all the glory. Without a second thought, the mouse turned and pushed the startled cat off the ox's back into the water. The mouse then stealthy crept up the ox's neck and hid himself inside the ox's ear. When the tired but triumphant ox finally reached the far side of the river, the mouse sprang from his ear and bolted forward towards the finish line. Sure enough, the mouse reached the finish line first and broke the victory ribbon.

The ox arrived second, followed by the tiger, then the rabbit. The rabbit had not won fourth place by his own merits though. He had hopped across the back of various animals until they reached the shore. Because the rabbit had run so fast, he had cut his lip and created a permanent cleft. The dragon flew over early for the race. The dragon's regular business was to control the South Sea. He shut down operations in order to attend the race. In his rush to complete his duties, he neglected his health and his ears got exposed to the harsh sea elements. The loud thunderstorm created a loss of hearing, so he became known as the Deaf Dragon. The snake was sixth to cross the finish line. Because his body was so long, the snake ran too fast towards the ribbon; all his legs were lost in the process. The horse was the seventh to cross the finish line. He was followed closely by the sheep, then the monkey, then the chicken, taking eighth, ninth, and tenth places accordingly. The three animals had found a piece of driftwood and ingeniously crafted it into a makeshift boat that ferried them across the river. As the monkey sat on the edge of the ferry, the fish nibbled the hair off his bottom. The sheep, overly excited by the game, stared relentlessly towards the finish line, damaging his eyes in the process. The dog came in the eleventh position. He could have come in much sooner, but he spent too much time frolicking in the water.

Finally, the pig came in, taking the twelfth and last position. The pig lost a lot of muscle tone in his legs during the race.

As the Jade Emperor God was presenting the awards, everyone was astonished when the soaking wet cat limped into view. Upon seeing the mouse, the cat stretched out her long, sharp claws and sprang towards it. The mouse, however, feeling exceedingly guilty at having cheated, did nothing to defend himself against the cat's attack. Instead of killing the mouse, the cat slapped his face so hard that his teeth became dislodged and protruded in the most obvious manner possible. Since that day, the cat and the mouse have been mortal enemies.

At the conclusion of the award ceremony, the Jade God commanded the twelve selected animals down to earth to represent people's birth years. From that day of the Animals' game of crossing the river, to this, people still consult the twelve animals' zodiac to interpret the meaning of each lunar year calendar in which a person is born. Each lunar calendar year is associated with one of the twelve animals that makes up and belongs to the circle of the zodiac.

Moral: Be fair in play with your friends and competitors. Do you know what kind of animal year you were born in?

32. Mr. Benevolence and the Turtle

Once upon a time, there was an animal lover known as Mr. Benevolence. So kind-hearted was he towards every living creature that he was careful not to step on an ant.

One day while strolling along the shore of a river, he happened upon a small turtle. He knew that turtles made excellent soup and, anticipating a tasty lunch, he put the turtle in a bag and went home.

The benevolent man's mouth salivated at the prospect of such a delicious meal, but he found himself in a quandary. He could not bring himself to kill the turtle. After careful consideration, he thought of a crafty way to lure the turtle into the pot of boiling water.

He placed a thin bamboo rod across the hot water. Then, smiling with cunning, he addressed the now terrified turtle:

"Dear turtle friend. I have heard that you are more nimble than a monkey. Show me how skillfully you can crawl across this bamboo rod. If you successfully make it to the other side, I will release you back into the wild."

The turtle knew that the man desired him for lunch. Retaining a small hope that he was sincere, he began his precarious journey across the bamboo rod. The turtle traveled with the desperate skill of the potentially boiled.

No one was more surprised than the turtle when he successfully made it to the other side.

Mr. Benevolence was disappointed. His stomach now beginning to rumble, he devised another scheme for turtle soup. Smiling broadly, he said,

"Excellent. You have a well-deserved reputation for nimbleness. Unfortunately, the rising steam made it impossible for me to see everything. Therefore, I want you to crawl over the bamboo rod again. If you succeed, I will place you back into the river."

Now the turtle became angry. He stretched his neck out and his eyes widened fully. Staring relentlessly into the eyes of Mr. Benevolence, he said,

"Excellency. Let us now discuss your reputation. You are known for benevolence and being kind-hearted towards animals. Yet, this game you are playing with me is a kind of torture that is far worse than death. If you are merciful then set me free. If you want to eat me, kill me now, and do it quickly. Let us not play this cat and mouse game any longer."

Mr. Benevolence was so ashamed by these dignified words that he forgot about his rumbling stomach and gently set the turtle free.

Moral: To know someone as he really is you must not listen to his words alone, but observe his actions as well.

33. A Fawn's Hard Lesson

Once upon a time, there was a man who lived upon the shore of a river. One day while he was hunting, he unexpectedly captured a gentle fawn. The hunter brought the fawn home hoping that by feeding him well he would grow into a fine deer.

Upon arriving home, several of the hunter's dogs rushed up leaping, barking, and salivating in anticipation of roast fawn cutlets for supper.

The gentle fawn was so frightened that he trembled fearfully in the arms of the hunter. Now the hunter was concerned that if he let the fawn roam with the dogs they might try to marinade him. Consequently, the hunter decided to have a stern talk with the dogs. "Now then, you pooches, listen well. This gentle fawn is my most favorite pet. You must conquer your appetites and instead protect this fawn for me. Do so and I will reward you with much more tastier meat."

Soon the hunter put the fawn together with his dogs. At first, the dogs were antagonistic towards the fawn, but, after a few days, they seemed to tolerate him.

Eventually the fawn grew up. Now a fine deer, his only problem was that he thought he was a dog. Consequently, the deer saw the dogs as his close friends. Now the biggest member of the pack, the deer constantly teased the dogs, carelessly kicking at them with his hind feet and licking their noses with his long, rough tongue.

Now secure in the knowledge that he was the strongest member of the pack, the deer became proud, bold and even reckless.

One day several of the dogs were in the street fighting over a bone. The reckless deer, observing the brawl, joined in hoping to secure the prize. The deer lashed out with his hind feet, sending two of the dogs flying backwards.

The rest of the pack, enraged by the deer's presumptuous behavior, remembered their earlier appetites for tasty fawn cutlets. Before the hunter could intervene, the pack of dogs had completely eaten the deer. Not until his quick death did the poor deer understand that he was not a dog after all.

Moral: Be alert. In some circumstances, your best friend can be your worst enemy.

III

Animal Fables

(Non-anthropomorphic)

34. The Hunter Who Blew a Bamboo Whistle

Legend has it that certain animals fear each other. For example, the deer is afraid of the raccoon, the raccoon is afraid of the tiger, and the tiger, in turn, is afraid of the bear.

Nowhere is this legend more evident than the story from ancient times about a hunter living in the South. This hunter specialized in successfully capturing small animals. He was skillful in playing a bamboo whistle to imitate animal sounds.

One day the hunter traveled up into the mountains; after selecting a prime location, he skillfully blew his whistle in imitation of a deer sound, "yoo...yoo." Unknown to the hunter there was a fierce raccoon nearby. The raccoon, hearing the sound of the deer, leapt out from behind a large boulder. Frightened, the hunter swiftly changed his whistle tone to imitate the sound of a tiger. The raccoon, terrified of tigers, leapt back behind its boulder, then quickly scurried away.

Unknown to the hunter, however, a real tiger lurked nearby and, thinking it had found a mate, quickly leapt towards the sound. Upon seeing the hunter, the tiger began to menace him. The hunter was so completely taken by surprise by the tiger that he dropped his bow and arrows unto the ground. With no time to lose, the hunter again blew on his whistle imitating the sound of a bear. When the tiger heard what he thought to be the fearsome roar of a bear, he quickly retreated into the forest.

Trembling in shock, the hunter bent to pick up his bow and arrows. Quite suddenly, a huge black bear strolled towards the hunter. Desperate, the hunter then blew his bamboo whistle in imitation of every animal sound that he knew. Unfortunately, there was no animal who could intimidate the fierce bear.

The hunter, now paralyzed with fear, closed his eyes and lay down on the ground ready to accept his fate. The bear, perceiving a tasty lunch, swiftly sprang upon the hunter. And that was the end of the bamboo whistle.

Moral: Before hunting, one needs to prepare for every contingency, have a back up plan, and never be afraid of animals in any circumstances.

35. Mr. Mouse and Mr. Cat

Once upon a time, there was a man who was very superstitious. Since he was born in the year of the mouse, he began to worship mice as if they were gods. Hence, he became known as Mr. Mouse.

In order to fully protect all mice, cats were forbidden from entering his home. Children were also warned that capturing mice in his home was forbidden. Mice were given free reign of his home. All day long mice could be found actively scurrying back and forth around his house. When other mice heard that Mr. Mouse so favored their species, they began moving into his house group by group.

Hence, the home of Mr. Mouse became known everywhere as an empire of mice. Eventually the mice demolished the home, having chewed everything from furniture to bed sheets. Mr. Mouse had to wait to eat the leftovers since the mice always ate their fill first. Mr. Mouse never slept well because the mice chirped and squeaked and scurried around all night long.

In spite of all that he had to put up with, Mr. Mouse was convinced that he was not treating the mice well enough and was immensely afraid of offending them in any way.

As fate would have it, several years later Mr. Mouse, through circumstances beyond his control, was forced to move far away. A new owner, therefore, moved in. The mice, believing that the new owner would favor them as much as the previous one, did nothing to change their emboldened ways.

The new owner, observing the control that hoards of mice had over his household, became enraged. In order to rid him of the detestable mice, the new owner brought home many large, mean, hungry cats. In order to give the cats complete control of the situation, the owner locked all the doors and windows and took the tiles off the roof of the house. Several people were also employed to join in the ensuing battle using every means to fight the mice including smoke and water.

Eventually all the dead mice were piled up and either buried or burned. Since then there was no longer any welcome mat for mice in that home.

Moral: Man is the only one who takes control of his own household.

36. The Dim-witted Seahorse

At one time, there were an abundance of seahorses living in the East Sea. When calm, the entire body of the seahorse was smooth and silvery-white in color. When agitated, small sharp fins would expand outwards porcupine-like. The seahorse propelled himself by a tiny but strong dorsal fin located at the base of the spine.

One feature unique to the seahorse species is the pregnancy of the male. The father carries the eggs and gives birth.

The fishermen considered the seahorse the most prized catch of the season. The tradition was to smoke the fish, thereby sealing in the flavor and preserving it as well. For these reasons, the seahorse was a lucrative export and one of the main natural economic resources for the fishermen.

The seahorse was not easy to capture. Only the most experienced and knowledgeable fishermen were able to successfully hunt it. The seahorse could habitually be found in the deeper waters far away from the coastline. Additionally, the seahorse hunt was very seasonal; the father only produced eggs in the interval between spring and summertime.

A brief window of opportunity for harvesting the seahorse occurred only when the male surfaced during this time.

The fishermen would carefully lay out exceedingly large nets, over one hundred feet in both directions. When the seahorse swam to the surface, he became entrapped in the relentless net. Since his dorsal fin allowed him to swim in only one direction—forward— he would continue his journey deeper and deeper into the trap until he reached the furthest end of the net and was unable to retreat backwards. The seahorse then becomes exceedingly frustrated. Frustration turned to rage. Rage manifested itself with his body, balloon-like, grotesquely bloating outwards. In this state, the seahorse took on the absurd appearance of a floating porcupine. Unfortunately, the spiky fins invariably entrapped themselves around the net thereby securing the capture of the seahorse.

Moral: Hard work is not enough to survive; work smart.

37. The Enraged Bachelor

Once upon a time, there was a bachelor who bought a home in the West. Desiring to take himself a wife, he spent his entire spare time and money renovating the home for his future bride. When completed, his dream home was perfect except for one annoying fault: it housed mice.

One evening when he came home from work, he was shocked to find that all his new furniture had been chewed and scratched by the pesky vermin. The only items which remained unscathed, were a cast iron pot and a copper water vat.

Now the bachelor became enraged. He stormed and stomped around his house searching for the hated vermin. They had all retreated into the walls for safety and he had no way of getting to them.

His wedding had to be postponed until he could get the house back into tiptop shape. This delay depressed him, so one night he consoled himself with a bottle of wine.

The bachelor then fell into his bed in a drunken stupor. It did not take long for the mice to emerge from the walls. The bachelor woke up to find the vermin scampering in the boldest manner possible across his bedroom floor. Enraged, he threw the empty bottle at them. As the bottle smashed against the door, the mice again retreated quietly into the walls.

The bachelor fell asleep. Then he had a terrible nightmare. In his dream, he felt something wet trickling down his face. He could taste blood in his mouth. He opened his eyes to find a horrible mouse chewing on his nose.

Now the bachelor's rage knew no bounds. Leaping up from the bed, he bolted into the kitchen to retrieve a handful of straw and some matches. He then returned to his bedroom and stuffed the straw into the mouse hole. He then lit the match to the straw. He repeated this procedure at every mouse hole he could find. Then he went outside.

He ran wildly around the circumference of the house and shook his fist in rage. Then he laughed hysterically at the sound of hundreds of screaming mice. Every last mouse died as the house burned to the ground.

The bachelor stood holding a cloth to his now throbbing nose and laughed spitefully. Suddenly dizzy, he lay down amid the ashes and promptly fell asleep.

Next morning the bachelor slowly awoke from his dream with a smile on his face. What a sweet dream to have all the mice burned to death. Feeling something crusty on his lips, his tongue darted out from his mouth and tasted blood. Confused, he slowly opened his eyes and sat up. His mouth now fell to his chest as he observed the broad sunlight beaming wickedly upon the ashes of what had once been his home.

Moral: Watch your anger. Do not let your anger's fire burn your own house.

38. The Burdened Rider

Once upon a time, there was a rider who dearly loved his horse. So extreme was his concern for the animal that he often went to absurd, if futile lengths, to ensure its comfort. One day several people in his village were witness to a curious sight. Sitting astride his horse, he precariously balanced a heavy load of luggage upon his own head. His right hand controlled the reigns, while his left hand steadied the heavy bundle upon his head. Dangerously swaying back and forth, it was the kind of balancing act that could only end one way: badly.

Concerned that he would topple over any minute, a passerby rushed up to him and asked,

"Sir. Why do you not load that luggage on the horse's back instead of your own head?"

Nonchalantly, the rider replied,

"Sir, my horse missed his feeding last night. I am concerned that he is not strong enough to carry so much weight. So I am carrying the luggage for him."

Moral: Sometimes our heart is in the right place but our brain is out to lunch.

39. Tiger the Mouse-cat

Once upon a time, there was a man who owned a strikingly beautiful Persian cat. The cat, who had orange, white and black stripes, was filled with vigor, drive and daring; for these reasons he was named Tiger.

One day several friends came to visit the man. The conversation inevitably drifted towards the cat. The man proceeded to outline the various reasons why he had named his cat Tiger. He went so far as to say that people could easily mistake his cat for a baby tiger that he had found in the mountains.

The first guest agreed that the cat was unique enough to warrant a special kind of name, but went further, insisting, "Your cat is so much more than just a tiger. Tigers are violent and terrifying, but they cannot mount the clouds and ride high in the sky like a dragon. For this reason, it would be more appropriate to name your cat 'Dragon-cat.'"

Another guest stroked his beard thoughtfully and said, "Nonsense. Everyone knows that a dragon is more vigorous than a tiger. However, a dragon relies on the clouds to fly. You should rename the cat 'Cloud-cat.'"

A third guest nodded his head is disapproval. "The clouds could cover the sky and block out the sunshine. When the wind blows, the clouds disappear from sight. This makes the clouds less powerful than the wind. You should, therefore, re-name the cat 'Wind-cat.'"

Yet another guest held up his hands and clucked in disappointment.

"No. No. It is true that when the winds blow the sky and earth may become encompassed in darkness. However, a high stone wall is strong enough to defeat the wind. In my opinion, you should rename the cat 'Wall-cat.'"

Finally, everyone turned to the man who had not yet spoken and asked for his opinion. "Gentlemen, your suggestions are all interesting, but none of them are right. You see the wall may stop the wind, but the mice may also damage it. After awhile, the foundation of the wall may become weak and the mice may make their homes in it. Therefore, I strongly suggest that the cat be re-named 'Mouse-cat.'"

Moral: Comparison should be logical and appropriate.

40. Requesting a Sick Leave for the Donkey

Once upon a time during the Tang Dynasty there was an acrobat. He entertained the Emperor in the Imperial Palace. The Emperor was greatly pleased with the acrobat's skill; as a reward he was promoted to the position of Minister of Culture. The new minister's work was quite simple: to manage the actors and actresses in the court.

Since his work did not require him to be at the Palace every day, his habit was to play chess with his friends. One friend in particular always received him with great enthusiasm and affection. After he dismounted from his Donkey, his host always commanded his servants in a loud voice, "Be quick in taking the Donkey into the backyard; give him plenty to eat."

He would stay with his friend all day and way into the evening. Sometimes his friend seemed very reluctant to let him leave. Indeed, he was greatly moved in his heart and believed his host to be the best of his friends.

On one such day, the guest and his friend were playing chess in their usual leisurely manner. Unexpectedly, a Royal Messenger arrived from the Palace. The Emperor requested that the guest return for an audience. He asked his host to immediately bring his Donkey around from the backyard.

The guest waited what seemed an inordinately long time, then finally went out to find the Donkey. From a distance, what he saw astonished him: the Donkey was drenched in sweat and breathing noisily. The host friend was also in a great rush to try and disassemble the animal from the millwork to which it had been harnessed. The guest suddenly realized why his host had been such a good friend, always concerned that the Donkey be taken immediately to the backyard, and insisting that the guest remain with him until well after dark. He said nothing.

The next morning he returned on horseback to his friend's home for a game of chess. His friend asked what had happened to the Donkey. With a cold smile on his face, the guest replied,

"I'm dreadfully sorry that my Donkey was unable to come today. He is currently on sick leave from working too hard for you."

Moral: To correctly assess a person's character, do not only listen to what they say but carefully examine what they do.

41. The Snake's Shadow

During the time of the Jin Dynasty, the prefecture of Henan was headed by a man named Mr. Yue. One day, Mr. Yue went to visit a close friend whom he had not seen for a long time. When his friend opened the door to greet him, Yue immediately noticed that his friend had developed a very withered appearance. Concerned, Yue asked,

"What is the matter with you? Why do you look so ill?"

His friend replied with an anxious look on his face,

"I wish you hadn't asked that. As you will recall, the last time I was in your home you offered me a glass of wine, but the moment I lifted it to my mouth, I noticed that there was what appeared to be a tiny snake swimming in it, although I couldn't be sure. When I returned home, I felt sick. Why was there a snake in the glass of wine, I asked myself?"

Yue contemplated the question for a long time, but finally got it. Hanging on the wall of his home was a serpentine looking bow tied around an animal horn. Could it be that somehow his friend had seen a reflection of the bow in the wine?

After returning home, Yue once again invited his friend over for a glass of wine. His friend accepted the invitation albeit somewhat reluctantly. Yue set up the table exactly as before, and when he poured the wine, his friend again saw a snake swimming in his glass. He screamed,

"There it is again, a tiny snake swimming in my glass of wine. Do you see it?"

Yue pointed to the serpentine bow, wrapped around the horn on the wall and said with a smile,

"No. It's just a reflection of the bow in your wine."

The guest examined the bow and the wineglass carefully, and then realized what had happened. An embarrassed, but relieved expression then appeared on his face. The friends smiled and, with much laughter, drank several more glasses of wine.

Moral: Don't be fooled by an illusion. To do so may lead to misfortune.

42. The Turtle Hog

At the very beginning of the Ming Dynasty, there was a particular area known as the Upside-down River in which the dykes habitually collapsed. The river often flooded submerging many of the surrounding homes. This habitual natural disaster became a real nuisance for the Ming Dynasty's first Emperor, Zhu Yuanzhang.

The Emperor finally assigned his Minister of River Defense to investigate the problem and arrive at a solution. The Minister discovered that the river flooded because beaver-like hogs were digging their horny snouts into the embankments and seriously damaging the dikes.

It was well known among the Emperor's inner circle that his family name "Zhu" also meant "pig" or "hog" in its pronunciation. For whatever reason, the Emperor had developed an almost pathological hatred for his name. It was an informal decree that if anyone referred to the abhorrent name he would be instantly killed.

The Minister of River Defense was disconcerted by this discovery and reluctant to convey the information to Emperor Zhu.

The Minister, in a dilemma as to what to say, and fearful for his life, considered his options. Eventually he decided to put the blame on the turtles. He chose this name because turtle referred to the name of the Yuan Dynasty which was overthrown by the Emperor Zhu.

Emperor Zhu, as expected, was delighted to learn that the turtles had caused the floods. He immediately issued a decree to have all the turtles captured and killed until none remained in any lake or river.

Since that day, no more turtles existed anywhere in the area. However, the beaver-like hogs flourished and the flooding increased steadily.

Moral: The semantics of politics can cause economic problems.

43. How the Brothers' Goose Got Cooked

Once upon a time, there were two brothers who enjoyed hunting together. Periodically, they ventured into the woods always hopeful of capturing bigger and better prey.

One day while hunting a deer, a lone wild goose came into view: it was very large and quite fat. Excited, the two brothers decided that the goose would be an easy kill. The younger brother said to the elder,

"What an easy target. After we shoot it, we will take it home and boil it for dinner."

The elder brother, annoyed that the younger had taken the liberty of telling him how the meal would be prepared turned, and said with some disdain,

"Twit. Everyone knows you do not boil a goose. You roast a goose. It's a duck that you boil."

Now the younger brother, disgruntled at being taken to task by his elder, stubbornly dug in his heels and pursued an argument. The elder, determined not to allow his younger brother to get the upper hand, grew equally quarrelsome. And so they bickered, back and forth, each refusing to give in.

Finally, they decided to take their dispute to an impartial mediator: an old wise man. When confronted with the question of the proper method to cook a goose, the old wise man replied,

"Cut the goose in half. Roast one half and boil the other half."

The two brothers were exceedingly happy with this ingenious solution. They hurried back to the place where they had left the goose. Unfortunately, the goose had not waited around to find out what the brothers would decide to do.

Moral: Seize the moment or lose the prize.

44. The Greedy Farmer and the Four Fearsome Beasts

Once upon a time, there lived a farmer who was harassed by a contentious fox. At his wit's end, he finally consulted an expert woodsman about how to rid himself of the pesky beast.

"The tiger is the King of all the beasts," explained the woodsman, "Once the fox sees the tiger, he will become immobilized with fear. He will lay upon the ground and wait for death."

The farmer was pleased with the idea, so he built a tiger skeleton out of wood and stretched a genuine tiger skin over the frame. He then placed the imitation tiger on the ground.

Sure enough the following evening the fox came to the farmer's yard to make trouble. When he saw the imitation tiger, he shook from head to tail and fell down in mortal fear. He remained in that position until the morning when the farmer easily captured him.

Several days later a wild boar made its way into the farmer's cornfield. It wrecked havoc with the growing crops. The farmer thus had the fake tiger moved into the cornfield hoping to score a similar victory as with the fox.

Sure enough the wild boar made its way again into the cornfield. When it saw the imitation tiger, it shook with fear and fell to the ground. The farmer, therefore, successfully captured this beast as well.

These easy captures gave the farmer an idea. He decided to forgo the tough life of farming and capture animals for an easy living.

Soon afterwards the farmer learned that a leopard the size of a horse had sauntered into his field. Perceiving yet another easy capture, the farmer gleefully rubbed his hands together. The experienced woodsman, however, offered him a warning,

"Do not try to capture the leopard with the fake tiger. The real tiger and leopard are kin. So the leopard has no fear of the tiger."

Now the farmer's heart, fixed with the idea of quick money and an easy life, became suspicious of the woodsman's motives. "He's afraid that I might try to muscle him out of the way." He thought. So the farmer completely ignored the woodsman's advice.

The farmer placed the fake tiger in the field. The leopard immediately came out from his place of hiding. Now the leopard is a very cunning animal and no fool. He knew that the tiger was a fake.

Without further thought, the leopard pounced on the imitation tiger and ripped it to shreds.

Now it was the farmer's turn to shake in his boots. He grew so frightened that he fell to the ground completely immobilized.

The leopard obtained an easy capture and a quite substantial and tasty dinner to boot.

Moral: When you have a good thing going, you must be prudent enough to know when to draw the line, otherwise, greed will destroy you.

45. The Priceless Tiger Fur

Once upon a time, there was a ferocious tiger who carried a man off in his fearsome jaws. The man's son, witnessing the horrible event, quickly snatched an axe and ran after the retreating tiger. As he came closer, he saw that the tiger had inflicted serious injuries upon his father: he was barely alive.

Now the son became infuriated and, with the superhuman strength of the severely outraged, raised the axe against the tiger.

The father, witnessing his son's savage fury, cried with his last breath,

"Son, be careful. Chop off the tiger's legs, but don't touch his body. If you do the hide will be worthless."

Moral: The love of money could cost you your life.

46. The Monk and the Pig-farmer

Once upon a time, an exceedingly legalistic monk made a living by twisting religious law to suit his purposes. One day as this monk was strolling through the market place, he came upon a farmer who was about to slaughter a pig. Perceiving an opportunity to promote his propaganda in public, he raised his arms high above his head and shouted towards Heaven, "Merciful Buddha, please stop this man from committing murder."

The monk now addressed the man while a curious crowd of onlookers gathered round, "Our religion forbids you to kill that pig; it is wrong to take another life. When the monks walk along the road we are always careful not to step on even a small ant, for that is also murder."

The pig farmer, confused by the holy man's words asked, "But it is not the same with the pig. It must be killed so that people can eat it and live."

"No," replied the monk vehemently. "Our religion teaches that you must never kill any living thing in any circumstances. Whatever you kill in this life you will be reincarnated as it in the next life."

The crowd of assembled farmers now grew uncomfortable. Every one of them had killed a beast for market. Now they grew worried about the state of their souls.

The monk, perceiving that he was winning them over to his way of thinking, then added, "If you kill a dog in this life you will be reborn as a dog in the next life; if you kill a sheep, you will be reborn as a sheep." Now he looked the pig farmer straight in eye, "And if you kill a pig, you will come back as a pig."

The pig farmer was an astute individual who saw through the false logic of the monk. Without any fear, he laughed and replied, "I think that I would like to kill a man."

The monk was shocked, then outraged, and, addressing the entire body of onlookers self-righteously shouted, "It is forbidden to kill even a cricket. Yet, this farmer says he would kill a man. Why would he want to kill a man?"

The pig farmer confronted the monk and loudly shouted for all to hear,

"You said that whatever we kill in this life we will be reborn as in the next life—that is why I would kill a man."

Moral: One should always think before speaking.

47. The Hunter King

There once was a King of Chu who liked to hunt though he was not very good at it. One day he and several escorts journeyed to the Cloud and Dream Lake. The official in charge of the Lake was flattered that the King had come here. Determined to provide the King with lots of prey, he shooed the birds and animals from the forest; they rushed out into the clearing.

The King was overwhelmed by the sight of all the animals and birds suddenly in his presence. He quickly lifted his bow and arrow and took aim at a small rabbit hopping before him.

Before shooting the rabbit, however, he noticed a rare sika-deer darting to his left. He quickly re-focused his aim to the left.

Before shooting the deer, he observed a glorious elk careening at his right. Shifting immediately, he again re-focused his aim to the right.

Before shooting the elk, though, he saw a beautiful white swan flying overhead. He quickly shifted his aim upwards. He was so dazzled by the beauty of the swan that he forgot to shoot.

The King finished enjoying the swan's flight and lowered his bow and arrow in search of other prey. Not only had the elk disappeared, so had the deer and even the lowly rabbit. No more animals or birds were in sight; they had all retreated to safety.

Moral: To be successful, one must focus on one's target and not be sidetracked by diversions.

48. The Tiger and Tang the Hunter

Once upon a time, in the South there lived a family named Tang. Every man in the Tang family was an expert hunter. Legendary hunting skills were passed on from generation to generation so that the eldest son always inherited the title "Tang the Hunter."

One Spring, a fierce tiger menaced the inhabitants of the mountain area outside of Jingde. Several hunters tried to kill the tiger but were themselves killed in the process. Finally, it was proposed to the County Chief that this was a tiger that only a Tang could kill.

A vassal was dispatched to the Southern region with bags of silver to recruit a Tang Hunter. When the vassal returned he reported to the County Chief, "Sir, the Tang family have agreed to do the job. They have selected two skilled hunters from within their clan; they will arrive here tomorrow." The County Chief was pleased to hear the good news. He ordered a special banquet be prepared in honor of the Tang hunters. The following day two Tang hunters arrived. When they were introduced to the County Chief, he was astonished at what he saw. The elder Tang looked so old that his hair and beard was stark white. An axe was tied around the waist of his long brown tunic. Bent over with rheumatism, he shuffled painfully with age. The other Tang looked so young that he appeared to be no older than twelve or thirteen. He was so thin and small that a soft breeze could knock him over.

Observing the two Tangs, the County Chief had serious doubts about their hunting abilities. He recalled that the fierce tiger had killed several local hunters, huge and strong as grizzly bears. With these uncomfortable doubts, the County Chief escorted his guests to dinner. The elder Tang, sensing his host's concern, inquired, "I was told that the tiger is only five miles away. Why don't we go now and kill it, then come back and have dinner afterwards?" The County Chief was surprised by elder Tang's confident proposal. Shrugging his shoulders, he said, "Hunter Tang, if that is your wish, I will have two runners accompany you to show you the exact location."

A short time later, the party of four, travelling along a mountain road, arrived at the mouth of a valley. Now one of the runners lost his nerve and began shaking from head to foot. "Why are you afraid my friend?" asked elder Tang, "we are here to protect you." As they progressed deeper into the lush valley, the second runner became as afraid as the first. He also began shaking uncontrollably. Elder Tang stopped and listened. Hearing nothing, he told younger Tang, "The tiger must be sleeping. Wake him up." Upon hearing these words, the younger Tang cupped his hands around his mouth and let out a fierce howling tiger roar. The sound echoed off the mountains and all around the valley. Hearing the imitation tiger roar reverberating around them, the two runners not only shook in their boots but their hair now stood up on end.

Next, the tiger slowly sauntered into view. In less than a second elder Tang stood before the fearsome beast. Planting his two feet squarely on the ground, he lifted the axe with both hands above his head, the sharp blade glistening upwards. Thus, he remained immobile as a statue. The tiger sprang its huge powerful body above elder Tang's head. Elder Tang's only movement was to tilt his head sideways. Then it was over. The tiger lay dead on the ground, his body slit fully from the neck down through the belly to the end of the tail. The ground turned red.

When they returned a short time later, the County Chief was overjoyed to see the carcass of the loathsome tiger. The size of the banquet was festive as all the people rejoiced over their victory. The County Chief then asked elder Tang his secret. With a smile, the hunter explained, "I was a student of martial arts all my life. For ten years, I concentrated on improving my vision skills. I spent another ten years strengthening my arms. I became so strong that I could remain holding a pole across my shoulders while two young men walked across it. I put so much effort into hard exercise that I got bored with it. I learned that it is easier to just wait for an exhausted opponent. All you really need is courage. That's how I beat the tiger."

Moral: Skill without courage is meaningless.

49. The Lost Horse

O nce upon a time, there was a man named Wang who lived in the Northern region. Wang was an unusually slow thinker. Once a year he loyally joined the armies of his Emperor, Gao, in a crusade to conquer the North.

For years, Wang rode the same red horse. One cold and frosty morning as the troops were preparing to mount and ride, Wang became exceedingly upset because a white horse was stabled where he had left his red one. Wang ran from camp to camp demanding that everyone search for his red horse.

The sun rose higher and the frost began to melt. Suddenly, as if by magic, Wang's red horse appeared. The frost, which had temporarily turned his red horse white, had melted. Wang did not realize this, joyfully explaining,

"My loyal red horse had a little adventure by himself, but returned back to me."

Moral: Don't be fooled by appearances.

50. The Scarecrow Fisherman

Once upon a time, a farmer cultivated a small fishpond. When a fish would grow to maturity the farmer enjoyed reaching a net into the pond and extracting a fresh fish to have for dinner. The farmer's only complaint was the annoying birds, who would fly in from the adjacent fields, swoop down, seize the smaller fish, and then boldly take off with their prize.

Since he could not guard his fishpond all the time, the farmer was hard-pressed to find a solution.

A neighboring farmer suggested that he try using a modified scarecrow. After all, he argued, if it works in the fields it should work in the pond.

The farmer, at his wit ends, decided that he would try it. So he took one of the scarecrows from his field and dressed it up to look like a fisherman, complete with a bamboo hat, jacket and fishing rod. He placed the scarecrow fisherman in the pond.

For the first few days the strategy worked splendidly. Birds circled above but were afraid of the scarecrow fisherman. As time went on and the fisherman never moved a muscle, the birds became bolder and began swooping down and seizing the fish at the edge of the pond. Eventually the birds understood that the fisherman was bogus. When understanding occurred they lost all fear and impertinently perched on the scarecrow's head and arms. Now the pesky birds were stealing more fish than ever from the pond.

Now the farmer, deciding that it was time for him to gain the upper hand, devised a plan borne from the mind of the totally frustrated.

One day when the birds were nowhere in sight, the farmer switched places with the scarecrow fisherman. A short time later, the birds began landing on his head and arms.

Reaching up the farmer seized two of the startled birds by their claws. Laughing, he said,

"The fake fisherman was a scarecrow who became a real fisherman. Tonight, therefore, we will be having water fowl for dinner."

Moral: Mixing the real with the bogus is a cunning and winning technique for gaining the upper hand.

51. The Snake with Legs

In the old days, there was a man who decided it was time for the younger members of his clan to try wine for the first time. So he gave them a small bottle to share. The youngsters discussed amongst themselves how they could evenly split the bottle. They argued that while there was not enough to go around, it would be unfair to give the entire bottle to just one person. They decided to establish a contest. Everyone would draw a picture of a snake; the one who finishes the drawing first wins. Every member of the clan immediately began drawing.

Finally, one young man completed the drawing first. With a cry of triumph, he snatched the bottle of wine and proclaimed his victory. He then boasted, "Not only have I finished first, but also I can add legs to the snake."

The young man's brother, having completed his drawing, stood up and, snatching the bottle of wine from his brother's hand said, "Everyone knows that a real snake has no legs. I have drawn my snake accurately—with no legs. Since your drawing is incorrect, I am the rightful winner and the recipient of the bottle of wine."

Everyone agreed that the second fastest winner was the real winner since his drawing was the more accurate. So, the wine had been given to him.

Moral: Complicating simple matters causes you to lose the contest.

52. The Closet Tippler and the Riverside Pigs

During the Tang Dynasty there was a great poet known as Su Dongpo. This poet loved holding dinner parties and enjoyed playing the role of gracious host to his guests.

One day he heard about a special kind of meat called "Riverside Pork." Apparently, when roasted with a honey-garlic sauce, the meat became so tender and sweet that it would melt in your mouth. Su, determined to achieve a reputation for excellent hospitality, decided that he must serve this meat at his next dinner party.

With this goal in mind, Su instructed his manservant to travel by foot to Riverside and bring back two prime pigs for roasting.

All went well with the selection and purchase, and Su's manservant began his journey home in the company of two fattened Riverside Pigs.

Unknown to Su, his manservant was a closet tippler. Hot, thirsty, and desperate for a drink, he stopped at a pub on the way home. Making sure the pigs were secure in a pen, the manservant then entered the door of the pub in great haste. It did not take long for him to pass out cold in a drunken stupor.

When the manservant woke up, he was horrified to discover that the Riverside Pigs had escaped from the pen. Breaking out in a fearful sweat, he rushed to and fro vainly searching for the Riverside Pigs. They were nowhere to be found.

Now quite desperate, he considered his options. There was not enough time to travel back to Riverside and purchase two more pigs. Afraid that his master would discover his secret drinking problem, he decided to purchase two local pigs and try to pass them off as the special Riverside ones.

The manservant arrived back at Su's home cold sober and with two fine, but ordinary pigs. Since Su had never seen a Riverside Pig, he had no idea that the manservant was deceiving him.

Overjoyed with his perceived luxurious acquisitions, Su rewarded his manservant with a bonus of new shoes and socks.

Su immediately organized invitations for a special dinner party featuring the famous Riverside Pork. The two regular pigs were taken to the back for slaughter.

When his guests had assembled, Su made an elaborate and ostentatious speech proclaiming the many excellent qualities of Riverside Pork. The dinner guests sat before their plates salivating as Su used words such as, "succulent, sweet, juicy and tender."

Dish after dish of the pretend Riverside Pork was served in a variety of ways. Chopsticks flew as every single piece was consumed with relish. The guests showered Su with an orgy of praise for this Riverside Pork. Everyone was thoroughly convinced that the meat from Riverside Pigs was excellent and entirely beyond compare.

Su blushed with sweet victory as the intoxicating words fell upon his eager ears.

Another servant interrupted the festivities to inform his master that a local villager was at the door and would like to see him. Su was in such a happy mood that he had the villager shown into the banquet hall. With a gesture of conviviality, and before all his guests, he asked the man what he could do for him.

All eyes were on the villager as he stated his business immediately,

"Forgive me for the interruption. I have found two Riverside Pigs rooting around my vegetable garden. Since I heard that your manservant had lost your Riverside Pigs and was hunting everywhere for them, I decided to return them to you right away."

These words fell on the assembly of persons like an axe on a chopping block. Still and silent, the atmosphere became stupefied. Everyone stared open-mouthed at the hapless villager. Shortly thereafter, the dinner guests left in an embarrassing silence and Su never did earn the reputation of "extraordinary host" he longed for.

Moral: Deceit comes naturally to a drunkard.

53. The Fat Cat

Once upon a time there was a man who suffered the indignity of having innumerable mice scurrying and rooting around his home. All night long the mice chewed and nibbled on the man's furnishings until virtually nothing remained intact. Additionally, the noise was so loud that the man had not had a good night's sleep in months.

Finally, the man decided to invest a great deal of money in a cat specially bred to kill mice. Lean, hungry and mean, the cat had the demeanor of a small tiger. Its eyes glowed red in the dark and when it mewed it sounded like the roar of a small lion. The mice were terrified of this salivating predator; they all hid quietly in the walls and would not dare venture out into the jaws of death.

For the first time in months the man slept peacefully during the night, and, during the day, saw no sign whatsoever of the pesky mice. So pleased and grateful was he with the cat that he began to spoil it.

Each day the man brought home fresh fish and tasty meat. The cat was always fed first and rewarded with the choicest cuts. The man made sure that the cat's food bowl was always full with every conceivable treat. The cat was also given the softest bed to sleep on, complete with many plump and fluffy velvet and silk cushions.

Eventually all the eating, sleeping, and continual pampering took its toll: the cat grew exceedingly fat and lazy.

The cat was now completely indifferent to the mice. Soon they began to venture out of the walls. Even worse, the cat had so much food to spare that he shared it with the mice.

Now the problem was double what it had been in the beginning. The man found himself in the middle of a household full of bouncing, scurrying, ravenous mice with a listless cat sleeping through all of it.

The man was now thoroughly disgusted with his fat cat. Seizing it by the scruff of the neck, he flung it outside. Standing in the doorway the man sighed,

"No where in the world can you find a good cat."

Moral: Too much pampering spoils the cat.

IV

Social Fables

54. The Two Braggart Brothers

Once upon a time, there were two brothers who were both boastful and shallow. Each thought that the other was more boastful than himself. They even nicknamed each other Brag and Flaunt. These two brothers married two sisters; this event made them all the more competitive. With each passing year, the brothers tried to outdo each other by acquiring new possessions. As soon as one bought something new, he immediately made it a point to boast about it to the other.

One day Brag's family bought a colorful new cotton quilt. Desperately wanting to show it off to his brother, Brag became frustrated because it was only used at night. In the day, his wife stored the quilt in a cupboard.

Pacing the floor and wringing his hands in frustration, Brag suddenly got an idea. Deciding that he had become ill, Brag took to his bed and covered himself with the handsome new quilt.

At the same time as Brag's bogus illness, his brother Flaunt had acquired for himself a new pair of hand-made socks. Flaunt, upon hearing of his brother's illness, immediately pulled on his new socks and went over to see him.

Rushing into Brag's bedroom, the first thing Flaunt noticed was the elaborate quilt spread out ostentatiously across Brag's bed. The second thing Flaunt noticed was that his brother was positively glowing with health and had never looked better.

Flaunt, determined not to be bested by his brother, removed his shoes and sat down on an adjacent chair. He then stretched his legs out fully so that his feet came to rest at a place uncomfortably near Brag's nose. Wiggling his toes, Flaunt pointedly ignored the quilt and stated bluntly,

"Well brother, for someone who is supposed to be ill, you look remarkably well."

Wringing his nose up in distaste, Brag pushed Flaunt's feet away from his face and off the bed. Smiling sardonically, he said,

"My problem, oh brother of mine, appears to be the same as yours."

Moral: A wealthy man usually does not have to boast, while a pretender will brag incessantly.

55. Lesson of the Taro Soup

Once upon a time in the Benevolence Creek countryside, there lived a simple peasant who cultivated taro plants. His plants were known for their large size and delicious taste. So exceptional were his plants that the local people dubbed him "Mr. Taro."

One night during a heavy rainstorm, a poor and threadbare student found himself sheltering in Mr. Taro's doorway. The boy, while standing in Mr. Taro's doorway, drenched with rain and shivering from head to foot; was all skin and bones. Mr. Taro's heart melted with compassion.

"Please come into my kitchen," said Mr. Taro kindly. "Take off your wet clothes and sit by the fire. I'm sure you are hungry. I will get you a bowl of hot taro soup."

The boy gratefully did as he was told. With a warm blanket wrapped around his shoulders, he snuggled up to the fire and eventually stopped shivering. He spoke weakly as he explained how he came to be in these circumstances.

"I come from a small village miles from here. I work as a laborer in the fields to save money for school. All my money goes to pay for books and tuition. I have no money left for transportation, so I have to walk to the capital to sit for the National Examination. The journey is taking longer than I anticipated. I stopped along the way to work, but now I have no more time to do that."

Blushing with shame, he then confessed,

"I ran out of food two days ago and have no money left to buy more."

The old man was filled with compassion for this hard-working boy, and, digging down deep into his soup pot, served up a heaping portion of his special homemade taro soup. The boy almost fainted with the hearty scent of the excellent food. As he tasted the soup, he looked at the man in amazement.

No words were spoken as the boy speedily ate the first bowl, then a second, then a third. When he was offered a fourth, he gave a lusty belch, apologized, then sheepishly declined more.

"That was the best food I have eaten in my entire life—it was a gift from Heaven."

Mr. Taro beamed with joy for he knew not only that his soup was delicious, but had been served to one who had known hunger.

Soon the rain let up and the boy was on his way. Before he left, he put his hands on Mr. Taro's shoulders. Facing him, his eyes welded up with tears and he said,

"Friend. I don't know what I would have done if you had not helped me. I was ready to give up. However, your excellent food and kindness have given me strength to continue on my journey. I am determined to pass my examinations. And I promise to someday give back to you what you have given to me."

With that, he was on his way.

Twenty years passed. Mr. Taro was now an old man still cultivating his famous taro plants.

The hapless boy who had desperately wandered into his kitchen had indeed passed his examinations. He had worked hard and overcome every obstacle which came his way. Now he was at the top of his professional career. People bowed before him and treated him with great respect. He had become the Premier of the Imperial Palace.

For years, the Premier had been served the finest and most exotic foods that money could buy. He had a team of gourmet chefs who cooked for him personally. Tasty delicacies were imported from far away lands. No one except the King himself was continuously served such excellent food.

Now the Premier grew tired of such rich gourmet foods. Every day he thought about the taro soup served to him by a peasant man in a humble cottage. His mouth salivated at the remembrance of it.

The Premier had to be sated. He ordered his chefs to prepare a bowl of taro soup. This they did with great pleasure. The Premier was overjoyed when the simple bowl of soup was placed before him. Lifting spoon to mouth, he inhaled its hearty scent, then began eating it. A look of disappointment passed over his face. Laying his spoon down beside his bowl, he declared that the Imperial chefs did not make it the way he liked it.

The Premier had to have his taro soup. There was only one person who made it the way he liked it. An envoy was immediately dispatched to bring both Mr. Taro and his soup to the palace.

Several days later an older but still healthy Mr. Taro stood before the Premier. Extending his hand in friendship, the Premier again thanked the old man for his kindness all those years ago. Mr. Taro had brought his special homegrown plants and promised to make the soup exactly as he had done on the night of the storm twenty years ago.

Salivating in remembrance of his youthful appetite for three large bowls, the Premier smiled joyfully as Mr. Taro himself placed a large bowl of the soup before him.

Lifting spoon to mouth, he inhaled the hearty scent then swallowed the soup. The Premier's brow creased as he tried a second, then a third spoonful. Finally, he pushed the bowl away from him and declared angrily,

"This taro soup tastes nothing like it did before. It is quite ordinary. In fact, my own chefs made it even better tasting than this. You have obviously forgotten how to make it."

Mr. Taro was disappointed by the change he saw in the once humble and grateful boy. The powerful man who sat before him was both contemptuous and condescending. With a boldness reserved only for the very old, Mr. Taro addressed the Premier,

"Forgive me, Excellency. I am an uneducated peasant and the only thing I know is the taro plant. I am stating quite honestly that what I just served you is identical to the three bowls of soup you ravenously engorged yourself with twenty years ago. When you arrived at my cottage you were starving and a cup of water looked wonderful to you. Now you have become spoiled from years of abundantly rich food. I would suggest that the change lies not with my soup but with your taste. In your climb to power, you have forgotten how to rejoice, just as you have forgotten how to taste the taro soup. I am an old man and not long in this world. I have seen many things. What you have forgotten on your relentless quest for power has not been limited to taros."

Before Mr. Taro could continue, the Premier interrupted him. Standing before him, he placed his hands on his shoulders and looked him straight in the eye,

"Friend. You are absolutely right. I humbly ask your forgiveness. I have been very inconsiderate. Please sit down beside me and allow me to honor you with the best banquet of your life."

Moral: One should not allow position and power to change one's character.

56. The Fragrant Orange

Once upon a time, there lived a King of the Liang State. He had a passion for citrus fruit, in particular sweet oranges. This King had tried every type of fruit available in the North. Now he became curious about the fruit in the South. Dispatching an envoy to the South, he instructed him to learn all he could about their fruit.

The people of the southern Wu State received this envoy in a very welcoming manner. The special fruit of the South, the envoy learned, was the orange. Huge baskets full of oranges were subsequently delivered to Liang the Northern King.

The King was delighted when he tasted the southern oranges. He declared them the freshest and sweetest he had ever eaten. He subsequently dispatched a second envoy to the South to see if there were any other kinds of fruit with an even sweeter taste.

The Wu people again welcomed the second envoy and happily sent the King several large baskets of "Honey Oranges." When the King tried the Honey Oranges, he was certain that they were even fresher and sweeter than the first ones.

Now the Northern King had convinced himself that there must be even sweeter oranges in the South. He wondered if the Southern people were greedy and did not want to share them.

In a duplicitous manner, he secretly dispatched a spy to the South. His mission was to find out if the Southern people were hiding and hoarding an even sweeter fruit.

This spy traveled all throughout the Southern State, passing through villages and towns in search of secret fruit. One day as he approached a small village, he perceived a sweet fragrance in the air. Unobtrusively sauntering around the village he noticed that every yard had the same kind of fruit tree. Huge, ripe oranges hung full and golden from all the branches. The air was thick with their intoxicating honey scent. The spy studied them carefully. They had the same appearance as the Honey Oranges though they were twice the size and emitted a heady fragrance.

The spy nonchalantly sauntered down the path to one of the yards, which housed the fruit tree. Pretending to be a merchant from the East, he inquired after the fruit. The owner gladly informed him,

"The fruit is called 'Fragrant Orange' and is indigenous only to the South. We cultivate it because of its beautiful golden appearance and its lovely scent. Unfortunately, it tastes bitterer than a lemon and refuses to sweeten even if soaked in sugar. It is entirely inedible."

These words thoroughly confused the spy. He refused to believe that anything so beautiful and sweet smelling could be bitter. Like the King, he had convinced himself that the Southern people were both hiding and hoarding this exquisite fruit. The spy returned forthwith to the King and reported all he had learned.

"Just as I suspected," said the King. "They are hoarding their best fruit for themselves and will not share it with us. The Wu people are greedy and stingy."

An ambassador was immediately dispatched to the South. There, he requested that negotiations begin for the export of their "Fragrant Oranges." The Wu King was astonished with the request, saying,

"The Fragrant Orange is bitter and inedible. Why not import Honey Oranges, they are sweet and wonderful to eat."

The ambassador was adamant. He wanted the "Fragrant Oranges" and nothing else.

Sighing with resignation, the Wu King ordered that several baskets of Fragrant Oranges be sent to the Northern King.

Delighted at having accomplished his mission, the ambassador personally escorted the Fragrant Oranges back to the North.

The Fragrant Oranges were brought into the great palace hall, where an enormous company of persons was assembled. Groups of people, dressed in their finest silks, drew up close to the King. The Northern King was overjoyed with the scent. His mouth watered in anticipation of this sweetly succulent fruit he had never before had the pleasure of eating.

The King stood before his now captive audience and, with a flourish, reached into the first basket and extracted a large, golden specimen. Caressing the golden beauty of the Fragrant Orange, the King slowly peeled off the skin. Separating several large juicy wedges from the fruit, he greedily popped them into his mouth all at once and proceeded to chew.

Suddenly the entire countenance of the King changed from overjoyed ecstasy to incredulous disbelief. His entire face wrinkled up like a prune and tears sprang forth from his eyes. Then, without any thought for propriety, the offending segments exploded from the King's mouth with such force that no less than six courtiers, five wives, four dukes, three monks, two princes and the ambassador were drenched with slimy projectile chunks.

"Water." Screamed the King.

"A dry cloth," was the communal wail of those drenched with the sour and now not-so-sweet smelling fruit.

Servants dashed to and fro trying to obey all the nobles at once.

The King was truly enraged. He was convinced that the Southern King had played a trick on him. Both ashamed and humiliated at the indignity of having lustily spat the not-so-Fragrant Orange pieces onto his repulsed guests, he immediately dispatched yet another ambassador to the South to denounce King Wu.

Instead of being offended by the Northern King's wrath, King Wu was actually amused by these events. He could only imagine the chaos in court as the King played the fool. Trying, however, to hide his amusement from the ambassador, he stated matter-of-factly,

"I explained to your prior ambassador quite explicitly that the Honey Orange is the best fruit of the South. I also explained quite clearly that the Fragrant Orange is bitter and inedible. If your King chose not to believe me, then whose fault is it that he made a fool out of himself?"

Moral: Greediness makes a fool out of even a King.

57. The Copper Buddha

Once upon a time, there was a lazy and worthless man named Bai. Bai refused to work for an honest living choosing instead to gain through deceit. One day Bai crept to the outskirts of his village carrying a small bundle in his arms. Arriving near the foot of a mountain, he stopped under an old pine tree. There, he unwrapped a tiny copper Buddha, stooped, dug a hole, then buried it under the tree. Satisfied, a crafty look passed over Bai's face as he turned and crept back to his village.

The following year Bai came by the burial site and noticed that it was covered with weeds. He then journeyed back to his home village and, gathering together many people, proclaimed with a mystifying gesture,

"You'll never guess what happened. I was returning home last night when I passed by the foot of the mountain and caught sight of a golden, twinkling object. Do you think, my friends, that I may have seen the light of Buddha?"

Bai's comments intrigued the villagers. They all followed Bai, and went to the foot of the mountain. Bai pointed to a patch of weeds and shouted:

"Look, there is a brilliant golden light. Can you all see it?"

The villagers peered intently but saw nothing.

Bai said again, more excitedly,

"There it is. Why do you not see it?"

The villagers rubbed their eyes and stretched their necks in an attempt to see the light, but all they saw was a clump of weeds.

Bai placed his hands over his eyes and said,

"I do not understand why you cannot see such a strong light. It is so bright that I have to shield my eyes from it."

After a moment Bai said with firm decision,

"All right. Since none of you have been able to see this apparently supernatural light, perhaps it does not exist and I am imagining it. Let's go back home."

Bai's deceitful strategy worked and the villagers thought that he was being truthful. They became concerned that they themselves could not see this apparently magnificent and supernatural light. Many become convinced that Buddha had granted a special ability to Bai, the mortal, to see the light.

The following day Bai was hanging out lanterns and decorating his home with brightly colored ornaments in celebration of his unique ability to see the light. Later on, he told of his plan to go to the foot of the mountain and find the source of the supernatural light.

A few days later Bai, accompanied by some villagers carrying picks and shovels, went back to the mountain. When word got out, pilgrims from neighboring towns and villages flocked there anticipating the discovery of the Golden Buddha, which, they surmised, must be the source of the miraculous light.

The villagers dug feverishly all around the clump of weeds, but found nothing. Bai then suddenly fell to his knees with a look of reverence on his face. With his eyes closed, he pretended to pray. He then took a shovel and dug where he had previously placed the copper Buddha. When he located the Buddha, he held it up for all to see. The entire throng of pilgrims then fell to their knees, kowtowing to the Buddha, like chickens eating rice from the ground.

From that day forward it became known far and wide that Bai had a supernatural Golden Buddha in his home. People from the surrounding district, even from hundreds of miles away, made a pilgrimage to see the Golden Buddha; there was an endless stream of people visiting Bai's home day after day.

Bai was happy to show the so-called "Golden Buddha" to visitors. He always kept it covered with rings of colorful silk, which he removed and gave to visitors. The visitors, in turn, donated large amounts of money to him. Bai thus became a very rich man.

Moral: Don't believe someone who is too showy.

58. The Careless Thief

Once upon a time, there was a country gentleman named Pendant who lived by himself in a modest cottage in a small village. A farmer by trade, he enjoyed a happy, easygoing life. Every evening he would visit friends and play chess and chat, returning home quite late.

In a neighboring village, a worthless rascal lived by thieving. One night this rascal was skulking by Pendant's home with a stolen fur under his arm. The rascal noticed that Pendant's gate was unlocked. Being the thief that he was, the rascal decided to double his take for the evening by robbing the farmer's cottage.

With the stolen fur still secure under his arm, the rascal jumped over the wall and slunk up to the door. As he was attempting to break the lock, he was startled by the sound of Pendant's creaking gate. In a sudden panic the thief leapt from the doorway and vaulted over the wall.

As Pendant strolled up the path to his home he was surprised to stumble upon a soft, lumpy object resting at the foot of his doorway. Reaching down to retrieve the object, Pendant held it up to the moonlight and was astonished to discover himself in possession of a luxurious fur. Realizing that a thief must have inadvertently dropped his ill-gotten gain, Pendant chuckled thoughtfully,

"So, he who tried to steal the chicken ends up losing the rice."

The owner of the stolen fur never was discovered, so Pendant spent the remainder of his days in possession of its luxurious softness.

Moral: Both the thief and the victim may end up losing at the same time.

59. The Monk and the Escort

Once during the time of the South Song Dynasty in the Su State, there lived a very worldly monk who did not follow the strict monastic rules for Buddhists.

This monk could often be seen frequenting pubs, publicly drinking wine and eating forbidden meat. When drunk, which was quite often, he became, mean, arbitrarily picking a fight with any individual who happened to pass him by on the street. His behavior became so bad that the Chief Executive of the Su State issued a warrant for his arrest.

Under arrest and officially charged, his punishment was permanent banishment to a remote frontier. A soldier was ordered to escort the prisoner across hundreds of miles of rough terrain to reach the frontier.

This soldier was extremely unhappy with the prospect of escorting a criminal across the barren land. So great, in fact, was his resentment that he took out his frustrations on the monk during the entire journey. A collar and chain were tied around the monk's neck and, yoke-like, he was forced to walk forward with the soldier pulling his chain from behind. From this position the monk was whipped, beaten, kicked, and punched. The whole while the soldier never stopped swearing a blue streak against his harnessed prisoner.

Every time a stick was laid to rest on the monk's now red behind, he bitterly cried out in pain.

One night they found themselves in a small village. The soldier was fed up with sleeping on the ground, so he decided to book a room at the inn for the night.

Viewing the inn with purpose, the monk conceived an escape plan. Smiling broadly, he addressed his escort,

"Escort, brother. You have indeed been hard done by, having to escort me all the way to the frontier. You have had a long and difficult journey and are very tired. I have been a very difficult prisoner, always crying and walking so slowly. I am deeply sorry for all the trouble I have caused you. I wish that I had some gift to give you for your troubles. However, I only have some silver coins in my pocket. Please allow me to buy you a bottle of wine to show my total obedience and understanding."

These words pleased the escort for two reasons. First, he was getting some well-deserved recognition for the awful job thrust upon him. Second, he loved to drink.

Hot, tired and thirsty, and anticipating the wine, the escort began to feel generous. He released the monk from his harness and unlocked the collar and chain from his neck. Then they both sat at a table and ordered an excellent wine.

Soon some tender and succulent meat was also placed on the table. The escort ate with gusto. All the while the monk made sure the escort's wine glass was never empty.

It did not take long before the escort fell over in a drunken stupor. When they were alone, the monk took out a razor and shaved the escort's head. He then quickly stripped off his criminal's uniform and exchanged clothes with the sleeping escort. When the scene had been set to his satisfaction, the monk took one last look at the escort, then escaped through an open window.

The next morning the escort woke up somewhat perplexed. His head throbbed painfully as he squinted against the sunlight shining brightly through the open window. Suddenly sitting bolt upright, he desperately searched the room for the monk. As the realization dawned on him, he broke out into a cold sweat.

Worse still, the escort found himself chained about the neck and wearing the criminal's uniform. A glance in a mirror confirmed the worst as he mournfully observed his baldhead.

Finally, he tried to rationalize his predicament. Gazing at himself in the mirror, he reflected,

"No, the monk has not escaped. He is right here. Where on earth am I?"

Moral: A drunkard has trouble finding himself.

60. The Magic Mosquito Repellent

During the summertime swarms of carnivorous mosquitoes relentlessly sought human blood. Bad enough in the daytime, nighttime became almost unbearable as people found it difficult to sleep while fighting the marauding invaders.

One man in particular had a passionate hatred for mosquitoes.

One day this man had occasion to travel to a neighboring village. There he noticed that a crowd had gathered around a small stage.

A man dressed as a Taoist Priest stood on the platform. He held a number of sticky yellow papers with winding red lines. The priest-like man was selling mosquito repellent. The man's eyes widened with intent interest as he listened to the seller's eloquent sales pitch.

Without stopping to think, the man promptly bought one of the "guaranteed" repellents. Thinking himself extremely fortunate, he went home.

That night he pasted the special paper on the north wall of his bedroom exactly according to the instructions. He then settled down comfortably, anticipating his first night's peaceful sleep all summer.

In the night, however, the mosquitoes invaded his bedroom in full force. When he awoke in the morning, he was swollen with red itchy mosquito bites from head to foot.

Furious, he snatched the useless repellent from his wall and set out to find the charlatan who conned him. Sure enough, the priest-like salesman was again on his platform and again repeating the same eloquent promises.

The man pushed through the crowd and grabbed the salesman by the collar and said, "You are a liar. Yesterday I bought your repellent and pasted it to my wall. Today, just look at me. I am covered with itchy mosquito bites. Your guarantee is worthless. I want my money back."

The salesman, extremely embarrassed and afraid of losing customers, refused to admit failure, "You did not apply it properly. You must have pasted it in the wrong place."

Sarcastically, the man asked, "Where should I have pasted it—in a mosquito net?"

Moral: Do not believe everything you have only heard.

61. The Burglar and the Fool

Once upon a time, there was man who was a complete fool. One day he was sitting at home with nothing to do but watch the tap drip. Suddenly he heard the sound of heavy boots trying to kick his door in. Before the fool could leave his seat before the tap, a burglar had kicked the door in and gained entry into his home.

Hurriedly, the fool scribbled a note, which read: "No entrance." He then pasted the note to the second door in his home. The burglar's response to the note was a few hard kicks to this door before it was also flung open.

The fool then retreated to his bedroom and pasted another note on the door, which read, "No entry beyond this point." Again, the burglar's response to the note was a violent kick to the door: it flung open immediately.

The fool, now fearful for his life, retreated into his bathroom and locked the door. The burglar, seeing the locked door, began kicking it.

The fool, quivering in the bathroom, suddenly conceived a brilliant idea to stop the burglar. Calmly, he said,

"It's occupied."

Moral: Do not anticipate respect from one who broke in.

62. Like Father, Like Son

In ancient times, there were no matches to light a fire. Two sticks were usually rubbed together to start one. One evening a man named Li was stung by a scorpion. His arm throbbing in pain, he called for his son to come quickly and make a fire for him. Li waited and waited and his pain grew worse and worse. Finally he screamed to his son,

"What's taking you so long?"

His son sauntered back to his father and replied,

"I've been looking everywhere for two sticks to rub together and can't find any. Now it's too dark to see any more." Suddenly his son had an idea,

"Father," he said, "If you give me a light from your fire I can continue searching for the sticks in the darkness."

From the light of his fire, Li looked down at his wounded arm and realized that the pain from the scorpion sting had subsided. Sighing deeply, he said,

"It was worth the pain to discover what an intelligent and loyal son I have."

Moral: If you have a light, you don't need to make a light.

63. The Digestion of the Pear and the Jujube

Once upon a time, there was a medical doctor who was dispensing advice about the digestion of food. "In the fruit category," he said, "the pear is good for our teeth but, if too much is eaten, it could upset the stomach and damage the spleen. The jujube, a fleshy edible fruit of the jujube tree with a large hard seed, works the opposite way. It helps the spleen and stomach but is bad for the teeth."

An ignorant man who thought himself knowledgeable decided to solve the problem outlined by the medical doctor.

"When we eat pears," he said, "we should chew them carefully, but not swallow them. By spitting out the chewed up pear, we help our teeth and save our spleen and stomach. Conversely, when we eat a jujube, we should by-pass our teeth and swallow it whole. This way, we help our spleen and stomach and save our teeth."

Moral: Knowledge can not be swallowed like a fruit. The digestion of fruit is analogous to acquiring knowledge. Students must be careful to chew on what they hear, and digest what they learn.

64. The Boy Learns Several Trades

Once upon a time, there was a boy who reached the age where he had to decide what he wanted to do with his life. Under the tutelage of a master, he became an apprentice umbrella maker. Many years later his training was completed. He was now a fully qualified umbrella maker. With a nice set of tools, he opened up his own umbrella making business. Unfortunately, he began his business at the beginning of the dry season when there was no market for umbrellas. Furious with his situation, he threw away his tools in a fit of rage.

He then heard that a lot of money could be made selling waterwheels. So he began an apprenticeship under a master craftsman. Many more years later he was a fully qualified waterwheel maker. Unfortunately, just when he opened his own shop to sell waterwheels, the wet season began. It rained day after day, week after week, months on end. The rivers flooded and all the canals and ditches were overflowing with water. The last thing anyone needed was a waterwheel.

So he decided to go back into the umbrella business. It took a long time, however, for him to re-assemble all the tools he had thrown out. Just when he had everything ready to begin making umbrellas, the sun began to shine again. Needless to say, no one bought an umbrella.

While he pondered his ill fate, a group of brigands stormed the village and began vandalizing and thieving everything in sight. Eventually the brigands were all captured and imprisoned. The event gave the man a new business idea: weapons. He perceived that the weapon business would be both easy and profitable and completely non-seasonal.

Soon he was again an apprentice to a weapon maker. Years later he was fully qualified. By the time he had learned the trade, however, he was too old to work. He no longer had the strength, hand-eye co-ordination or stamina to forge a sword with a sledgehammer. All that was left for him to do was sigh with regret.

Moral: One needs to be far-sighted with one's goals. Shortsightedness will result in wasted time.

65. The Rich Man, the Knight, and the Beggar

Once upon a time, there were two men who were the very best friends; one was named Zhang the Third, the other Li the Fourth. These men were snobs and very class conscious. They even addressed each other as Third and Fourth.

One day when they were strolling through the market place, a luxurious rickshaw came into view. Inside the black and silver carriage sat a man elaborately adorned in the red velvet and softest gold silk. The man had an exceedingly large head out of which two large ears grew elephant-like. No less than twelve servants, three in front, three in back, and three on either side escorted the vehicle. This retinue was intimidating indeed.

As the large group approached, Third pulled Fourth over against the wall yielding the way to the enormous carriage of persons. Both men sucked in their breath as the group brushed within an inch of their bodies. Finally expelling their breath, Third smiled and said to Fourth,

"I had to push you against the wall because the man in that carriage is a close relative of mine. If I had not yielded the way to him, he would have stopped, stepped out and bowed to me. I did not want to hinder his journey. It's better that he did not see me."

Fourth nodded his head in agreement and said,

"Oh, you did absolutely the right thing. Your consideration for other people shows your good breeding."

Pleased with these words, Third smiled broadly and the two men walked on.

As the road curved, a Knight, arrayed in shining silver armor, was astride his magnificent black stallion. The horse was adorned with gold and red silk blankets and wore a huge white plume on its head. A crest on either side of the blanket denoted nobility. The Knight was escorted by several servants, all of whom rode with the speed and might of the unyielding. It was an even more intimidating sight than the rich man in the carriage.

Third quickly pulled Fourth over into the doorway of a house. There, the men briefly sheltered as the horses galloped by so closely that pebbles and dirt particles were flung on both men.

As Fourth began dusting the dirt off his clothes, Third smiled even more broadly than before. Patting his friend on the back, Third said,

"I pulled you into this doorway because the Knight on that horse is a close friend of mine. In fact, as children, we were brought up together. He is like a brother to me. If I had not yielded the way to him and he had seen me, he would have dismounted and promptly dragged me off with him for a meal in a fine restaurant. That would not have been very convenient for you, my friend."

Fourth smiled as well and said,

"Your consideration knows no bounds. This nobility of soul shows that you have been very well brought up indeed."

The two friends sauntered on. At a crossroads, a beggar approached from the opposite direction. He wore filthy rags. His hair was long and matted with dirt. His skin gave the darkened appearance of never having had a wash in his life. On his feet were two different shoes, both old and dilapidated. Since Third and Fourth were up-wind of the beggar, the combined stench of stale wine and the unwashed assaulted their nostrils in a most unpleasant manner. Moving closer towards them, the beggar held out his hand. Hiccuping, he pleaded in an alcoholic slur,

"Money to the poor. Be merciful and give money to the poor."

Now it was Fourth's turn to pull Third over behind a tree. The two men hunkered down behind the sheltering leaves until the beggar had passed by.

Baffled, Third asked Fourth,

"Why did we yield the way to that beggar?"

Fourth, smiling replied,

"That beggar is a close friend and a close relative of mine. If we had not yielded the way and hidden from him he might have recognized me."

Shocked by this admission, Third asked,

"I had no idea you had such a poor relative—why did you admit it to me?"

Fourth, smiling sardonically, replied,

"All the rich and noble men have already been taken by you. The beggar was all that was left over for me."

Moral: People will see through our social pretensions.

66. Archery Expert Bested by Oil Seller

Once upon a time, there was a man named Chen who lived during the Dynasty of the Northern Song. Chen was an expert at archery. Indeed, his skills were so superior that he had no rivals to speak of.

Many onlookers always followed Chen to his target practice. Dazzled, these spectators always surrounded the field and cheered whenever Chen shot his arrow from his bow.

One day one old man who sold cooking oil for a living found himself at the target practice area. The old man slowly lowered his pole from his shoulders and stood observing Chen along with the other spectators.

Whenever Chen was in the presence of an audience his movement became more elaborate and contrived. With a flourish Chen reached for his arrow, inserted it into the bow and carefully took aim. The arrows flew from Chen's bow like the wind. Eighty per cent of the time the arrows pierced the bull's eye. The crowds of onlookers cheered more loudly with every success. All except the old man; he only slightly nodded his head in recognition of Chen's prowess.

The old man's lack of response did not go unnoticed by Chen. Insulted, Chen leaned disdainfully towards the old man and loudly inquired,

"Do you know how to shoot an arrow from a bow? Do you not think that my archery skills are excellent and worth recognition?"

The old man smiled humbly and replied,

"I do not know how to shoot an arrow from a bow. Your skills at archery are the result of years of practice. I am, however, somewhat disappointed in your archery skills. In spite of all the practice, you are not an excellent shooter, only a mediocre one."

These words of honest assessment provoked Chen's wrath.

"You ignoramus. You, who admit to knowing nothing about archery have the effrontery to insult me."

The old man spread his hands in a reconciliatory gesture. Speaking mildly, he replied,

"Please do not be angry with me. I was not trying to insult you, only to tell you the truth. I am an ordinary peasant man who knows nothing except one thing: how to sell oil. After years of practice, I do it very well. Please allow me to demonstrate."

The old man placed an empty oil bottle on the ground. He then placed a copper coin with a square hole in its center on the mouth of the bottle. He poured oil from a solid mound through the center of the coin down into the bottle. As the bottle filled to the brim, the copper coin remained clean with not a spot of oil on its surface. Not one drop of oil was wasted, as the solid mound was wrung dry.

The crowd of spectators was astonished by this feat of expertise. They broke out into loud applause and praised the thrifty talent of the oil seller.

In response to their praise, the old man smiled and replied humbly,

"I have no special talent at all. My special skill is simply the result of years and years of practice, that is all."

Chen, upon observing the old man's skill and hearing his explanation, was left with nothing to say.

Chen, the archery expert, and the old man, who sold oil, bade one another good-bye and went their separate ways.

Moral: Every field of endeavor has its own resident expert.

67. Folk Prescription Liu

During the Song Dynasty there was a medical doctor named Liu. He was skillful in administering herbal folk remedies to his patients. For this reason he became known locally as "folk prescription Liu."

One day Su Dongpo, the Great Court Poet, paid Liu a visit. While they were speaking, a patient arrived in need of immediate care.

"What is wrong with you?" asked Liu.

The patient replied, "I have been blown by the wind as if on the sea in a boat. Now I feel frightened all the time. Can you cure me of my fear?"

Liu took a moment to contemplate the remedy before replying,

"You must return home and find the handle from an old boat. Dry it in fire. Then put it into a dish. Add some cinnamon and some poris cocos, and then grind it all into a fine powder. Boil it then drink it. After this you will immediately recover."

The patient knew that both cinnamon and poris cocos are analgesic treatments. However, he could not understand how the handle from an old boat came into it.

Liu, placing his thumbs importantly in his vest pockets replied proudly,

"The old boat handle is the key to the miraculous cure. The handle contains the sweat from the hands of the fearless seaman. Such a man would be skillful in fighting the wind and the waves. Therefore the sweat from such a man will cure you of your fear."

Now the Court Poet Su had been attentive to all these things. Unable to contain himself any longer he broke down into convulsive laughter. Finally regaining his composure, the poet inquired of the doctor,

"Tell me something. A member of my family has recently been ill. Every night he sweats so much that three heavy blankets become drenched. What kind of medicine would you recommend for this kind of problem?"

Without thinking, folk prescription Liu replied,

"This problem is easy to cure. Find a few palm leaf fans. Dry them and grind them into powder. Add water to the powder. Then have the patient drink the mixture: this will cure the sweats."

The poet, smiling at the advice replied,

"According to your prescriptive pattern then, it logically follows that if we burn a brush and ink together until they become ash and have an illiterate person drink it, then this person will be able to write. Further, if we ask an ugly man to smell the earring of a beautiful woman, then he will become a handsome gentleman."

Moral: Never trust a folk prescription; it might just waste your time and lighten your pocket book.

68. A Calligrapher's Indulgence

During the time of the Tang Dynasty, there was a celebrated calligrapher named Ouyang. His work was habitually praised by other calligraphers for its polished style and strict structure. A legend arose as to the way in which Ouyang achieved such superior craft.

When he was quite young, Ouyang embarked on a journey by horseback. While travelling down an ancient road, he noticed a side path, which was covered with moss and weeds and greatly overgrown. Attracted to the strange wild beauty of this less traveled path, he decided to explore what he perceived as a seemingly forgotten place. Ouyang proceeded along the path until he reached the end where he encountered an ancient gate.

Ouyang dismounted and strolled over to the gate to observe its configuration. The gate was greatly weathered and in need of serious repair. However, Ouyang was astonished and delighted to discover that the center of the gate was still intact. Even more astonishing was the inscription, which was still legible. Ouyang was surprised that he recognized the work as that of a great calligrapher from the old Dynasty. The inscription appeared to be a dragon invoking storms. Such was the singular uniqueness of the feature that no ordinary calligrapher could imitate it.

Ouyang was both dazzled and entranced by the beautiful inscriptions on the gate. Reluctantly, he mounted his horse and turned back towards the main road. Halfway down the path, however, Ouyang was compelled to turn back towards the gate for yet another look. He ran his fingers over the characters and carefully studied all the curves and lines.

As darkness began to fall Ouyang was unwilling to leave in spite of his fatigue. The moon rose in the sky and he continued to observe the characters by its light.

Finally, Ouyang was fully satisfied that he had thoroughly studied every aspect of the beautiful calligraphy.

Content, he mounted his horse and departed from the ancient gate.

Moral: In order to excel at any craft, one needs to thoroughly focus on the study of it in an all-inclusive manner.

69. The Swollen-headed Student

Once upon a time, there was a man named Bo Le who was an expert at appraising horses. Late in life, he published a book entitled *Experiences and Instructions on Equine Appraisal.* Bo Le's book outlines specific methods by which an individual may accurately appraise the value of a variety of horses.

When Le had reached old age, he called his eldest son to come and see him.

"My son," he said, "This book is the summation of all of my knowledge about horses based on a lifetime of observation and research. It is absolutely seminal in its field; there is no other like it. For this reason, I want you to study it thoroughly so that you will inherit my knowledge and reputation."

Le's son was happy to accept the book and very much liked the idea of becoming famous like his father. For the latter reason, he was diligent in his study and worked day and night at memorizing it. Through the self-disciplined routine of the highly motivated, he soon had the book completely memorized.

Although Le's son was self-disciplined and had a good memory he also had the unfortunate character trait of pride. Now that his head was thoroughly swollen, he convinced himself that his father's life experiences had been superficial. Further, he believed that he could become even more famous than his father could in half the time. He decided to achieve this goal by finding the one horse his father admitted in his book to never being able to find.

"Father, I have memorized your book. Now I intend to go out and find the elusive 'winged steed' of which, you write."

Smiling at the boy's reference to the mythological beast, Le was, nonetheless, happy that his son was showing a genuine interest in inheriting his knowledge.

"Good," said his father, "That is the first stage of your learning experience. I wish you well on your journey."

So the boy prepared for his trip. He packed food, clothes and Le's book in a knapsack, then set out on foot in search of the elusive "winged steed."

The boy remembered the traits of the animal:

1. A bump on his head.
2. Two protruding eyes.
3. Hooves that look like pies piled up.

With the three points memorized, the boy began searching diligently for the steed.

Venturing into a pond, the boy found an exceedingly large and ugly toad croaking loudly on a lily pad. At last, he thought, the "winged steed."

The boy was overjoyed with the knowledge that he had discovered in days what his father had been unable to discover over the course of a lifetime.

Placing the toad carefully in his knapsack, the boy bolted home, all the while imagining how respectfully everyone was going to treat him because of his brilliance.

When the boy came before his father, he held the toad in an arrogant manner beneath his father's nose.

"Look father, I have found the 'winged steed' in no time at all. This is just the beginning. From now on I am the resident equine expert in the household and I will be in charge of all things concerning horses."

Rage over the ludicrous pride exhibited by his son finally gave way to laughter as Le considered the irony of the situation, saying,

"Your 'winged steed' may be capable of jumping, but try harnessing him to a cart."

Moral: Pride at a good memory is ridiculous; only practice will allow one to obtain genuine knowledge.

70. The Quack Surgeon

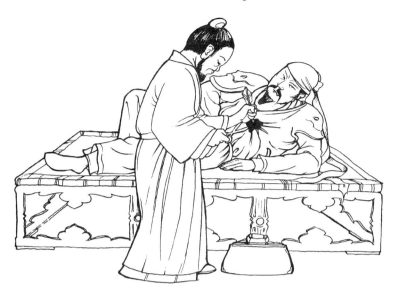

Once upon a time, there was a man who pretended to be a doctor but who had no knowledge of medicine. He had inherited the title of "medical surgeon" from his ancestors. This quack incessantly bragged that he could cure any kind of injury or disorder.

One day a military General was brought into the surgery; he had been shot in the chest with an arrow. Since half of the arrow was in the General and half was sticking out, the quack had no time to lose. Reaching into his medical bag, he extracted a pair of scissors and cut off the piece of arrow sticking out of the General. He then performed an elaborate application of wrapping bandages around the wound. After thoroughly taping up the bandages the quack placed his open palm before the General and asked to be paid.

The General, in pain and somewhat confused, weakly asked,

"What about the other half of the arrow still stuck inside me?"

A rather stern expression grew on the quack's face and he replied pompously,

"The treatment of internal injuries is the job for a physician. I, as a surgeon, only treat external injuries."

Moral: An operation sometimes needs to be performed on the brain of certain surgeons, for there is evidence of serious malfunction there.

71. The Water Chestnut Tree

Once upon a time, there was a man named Bei who lived in the North. Since chestnuts only grow in the waters of the South, Bei had never seen one.

One day Bei had the opportunity to travel to the South. When he arrived there, he was invited to the home of a friend for dinner. Bei's friend, desiring to be a good host, decided to serve a specialty: water chestnuts.

Bei examined the chestnut carefully, before popping it into his mouth. As he began to chew, the nut seemed to get harder not softer.

The host, now aware that Bei knew nothing about chestnuts, exclaimed,

"My friend, the water chestnut has an exceedingly hard shell, you must first remove it before eating the nut meat inside."

Bei's face burned with shame and he felt embarrassed at what he perceived to be his ignorance and lack of sophistication. He decided to regain lost ground by pretending that his actions had been deliberate.

"Of course I realize that the shell is usually removed. I ate it with the shell in order to aid my digestive system."

Now the host was insulted that Bei had resorted to lying. Determined to best his friend, the host inquired,

"Since you are so familiar with them, you must have chestnuts in the North, then?"

"Of course," replied Bei quickly. "They are in abundance everywhere, stands of chestnut trees surround the mountains."

Moral: Lack of knowledge is nothing to be ashamed of; one can always learn. The problem arises when one pretends to know something that one does not.

72. The Sour-tasting Wine

During the years of the Eastern Zhou Dynasty, many battles raged between the surrounding Six States. Towards the very end of this bellicose period, a famous politician named Su Qin emerged. The Emperor Zhao was so impressed with Su's abilities as a politician that he rewarded him with the territory of Wuan. Su spent most of his life campaigning and ultimately winning the nomination for every state in which he ran. Su's ultimate victory was in obtaining the title of Premier and succeeding in ending generations of warfare by uniting all the Six States. He went down in history as one of the most powerful, influential and beloved of all politicians.

However, the road to Su's success was not always a smooth one. One day early on in his career, Su returned home after a long and arduous political campaign. Weary from overwork and extensive travelling, Su received a very cool reception from his family. His sister-in-law refused to cook for him, his parents refused to speak to him, and his wife did not bother to leave her weaving loom in order to welcome him home. They were united in believing that Su's long absences from home were achieving nothing.

One day the whole family gathered at the home of Su's parents in order to celebrate their wedding anniversary. As tradition would have it, Su's older brother respectfully presented his parents each with a goblet of wine he had made himself. His parents smiled and nodded their heads in approval, then drank all the wine in their goblets.

"Excellent wine my son," his father said. "The best wine I have ever tasted," said Su's mother to his older brother.

It was now Su's turn, as the second son, to present his wine to his parents. His mother and father both frowned when he offered them each a goblet. Refusing to even accept a taste, Su's father told him,

"Keep your wine you worthless good-for-nothing. I don't want it."

Then Su's mother, equally perturbed added,

"I will not drink your sour wine on my anniversary."

This time Su's wife shared her husband's shame and embarrassment at the insult. Hurrying over to her sister-in-law, she begged her for some of the homemade wine which Su's parents loved so much. Returning to her parents-in-law, Su's wife bowed respectfully and offered them the wine.

This time, Su's parents accepted the wine goblets in their hands, but still refused to drink the contents. Su's mother sniffed disdainfully, and, wringing up her nose said,

"This wine smells sour. Drinking this is sure to cause gas."

Su's wife did not receive this new insult well.

"That is ridiculous," said Su's wife. "I just now obtained this wine from my sister-in-law; it is the exact same wine you so recently proclaimed as being the best you ever tasted. How could it have turned sour in a matter of minutes?"

Su's father replied in a stern voice,

"You useless wife of my useless son. Even if it were a good wine, after you touched it, it must have turned sour."

Moral: It is not wine but familial relationships, which may become sour.

73. Pork as Punishment

L iving during the time of the Five Dynasties, there was a prominent official by the name of Li. This official was known for two strange quirks: firstly, he had an exceedingly ill temper and, secondly, he was unable to eat pork because after just one bite he would throw it up.

One day as Li was departing from a business meeting he noticed that two of his servants were engaged in a street brawl. Outraged by the unseemly behavior exhibited by members of his household, Li decided to make an example of them by punishing his servants in the most severe way possible.

Li spent hours stewing in rage. He decided that the various usual punishments such as flogging were not torturous enough. Li finally decided on the ideal punishment. Grinning with malevolent spite, Li implemented his plan of torture immediately.

The kitchen staff were instructed to prepare a plate full of pancakes and a large bowl full of roast pork meat. Li then ordered the two offenders to kneel down opposite each other and to eat up every bit of the pork.

The servants were confused but delightfully so at the prospect of such an unusual punishment.

All the while, as the servants obediently consumed the pork, Li ranted and raved about the brilliant success of his ideal punishment. He loudly proclaimed to his entire household,

"Behold. This is the punishment for anyone who steps out of line. Furthermore, if anyone else disobeys me or makes trouble for me, you will be additionally punished by eating an entire bowl of roast pork meat balls."

Moral: One person's idea of a punishment might be another person's idea of a reward.

74. The Listening Chess Player

During the Tang Dynasty, there was a famous chess player named Wang. For ten years he had stayed at home learning the art of chess. Eventually he began playing with chess players in his neighborhood and surrounding communities. As expected, Wang won all of the matches; no one could beat him. Because of all of his successes, Wang became smug. Certain that he could win the national championships, Wang packed up and began a long journey to the capital city of Changan.

One day just before dark Wang arrived in a small village. Weary with fatigue Wang wandered to the center of the village in search of lodgings. Wang became overjoyed when he noticed the sure sign of an inn—a red ribbon attached to a bamboo strainer hanging on a door. Gratefully entering the inn, Wang was warmly received by the innkeeper, a gracious old lady who ushered him into a clean, warm room. He was so weary that he ate some food in his room, quickly washed his feet in warm water, then sunk into bed preparing for a good night's sleep.

All of the rooms in the inn were separated by paper thin walls; when people spoke in one room they could be heard clearly in the next. As Wang blew out his candle, he could not help listening to a conversation between the innkeeper and her daughter-in-law.

"What a long night it is. I really can't sleep. Why don't we play a game of chess to pass the time," said the old lady.

"That's a good idea," replied the young lady, calling from another room.

"I've set up my board and made the first move. Now it is your turn," said the old lady, as she started the game from her bedroom.

Thus, the game went on, with each chess player in a different room calling their moves back and forth to each other. Finally, the old lady called out triumphantly,

"You've lost, my dear daughter."

"Yes. You have beaten me this time, my dear mother."

Wang remembered by heart all of the chess moves the players had made before falling into a deep sleep. The next morning he reviewed the moves on his own chessboard. Wang was astonished to discover that these simple women were more knowledgeable about chess and, their strategies more superior, than even his. From that day on, Wang never boasted about his chess prowess again. He discontinued his journey to Changan, and returned home where, with the diligence of the newly humbled, he pursued his study of chess with renewed fervor. In time, his efforts paid off and he became the master chess player of his generation.

Moral: *In order to succeed, we need to study harder and learn knowledge from those lesser than ourselves.*

75. Yu Flatters the Emperor

One day the First Emperor of the Tang Dynasty was walking in the Imperial Garden escorted by an official named Yu. The Emperor noticed a beautiful peach tree bearing bountiful fruit. Stopping to admire the tree, he lingered there for the longest time, exclaiming incessantly, "Oh, how beautiful is this peach tree."

Upon hearing the Emperor's comments, Yu approached him smiling and said,

"You are very observant, Your Majesty. Thank your good fortune that it is only in the Imperial Garden where this rare tree may be found; another like it has not been seen for centuries. It is indeed a special gift from Heaven to Your Majesty." Further, Yu said,

"It is only under your protection that this tree has become so strong and beautiful. Not even in heaven is there a tree such as this."

The smile on the Emperor's face disappeared as suddenly as it had appeared. His eyes penetrated through those of Yu, and he said,

"In the past someone often reminded me to keep a cautious distance from people who flatter me, just to win my favor. I used to wonder if you may be one of those people, but now I realize that, without a doubt, you are an insincere flatterer of the worst kind."

Moral: Insincere flattery will expose itself.

76. An Artist Views a Picture

Once upon a time during the Tang Dynasty there was a famous painter named Yan. One day, before Yan became known, he had an opportunity to view a unique painting by the great artist Zhang. The painting hung on the wall in a remote temple but, despite this inconvenience, Yan, in order to fulfill a promise to himself, made the journey to the temple.

On the first day, Yan viewed the painting briefly and in a superficial manner. His impression was that the work was so ordinary that it did not live up to Zhang's excellent reputation.

The second day Yan viewed the painting for a long time. He became aware that the work had more merit than he had initially realized and that, in retrospect, Zhang might be a good artist after all.

That night, after retiring to his bed in the inn, Yan was unable to sleep. He continued to contemplate the painting and his mind was filled with its every contour. Excited, Yan was determined to go back to the temple and view the painting yet another time.

In the early morning of the third day, Yan again entered the temple. He meticulously perused the painting noticing every detail including its structure, color, the characters, and their vivid expressions. He then came to the realization that it was a perfect work of art saying,

"This is a painting truly worthy of Master Zhang's reputation."

After standing in the temple for a long while, Yan collapsed into a chair still keeping his eyes on the picture. He eventually lay down on the floor and continued to look on.

Yan remained in the temple for two weeks, watching the sun sink in the west and the moon rise above the mountains in the east, never wanting to leave the perfect picture's presence.

Moral: A dedicated student must progress from a love to a passion for his subject.

77. The Greedy Water

Once upon a time there was a famous well of spring water called "greedy water" located in the city of Guangzhou. It was said that if a person drank water from the well, then that person would become greedy. This transformation would occur even if that person had never been that way before. After having drunk from the "greedy water," the victim would subsequently develop an insatiable desire to possess everything.

The spring water was clear and most appealing to the senses, however, because of its infamous reputation, no one would drink "greedy water." Even the neighbors went elsewhere to bathe and to obtain drinking water.

One year, the Guangzhou prefecture hired a new chief officer named Wu. After his arrival in the area, Wu heard about the spring and went to see it for himself. When the residents in the area heard of Wu's visit to the infamous well, they also went there.

In the presence of all, Wu scooped up a ladle of water and drank it. The people were astonished and looked at each other in dismay. This man had a reputation for honesty and fair play, but they all wondered if he would now be unscrupulous and corrupt, having drunk from "greedy water."

Although Wu was calm and confident, he could not help seeing the concerned look on the people's faces; he then recited a poem to them:

> There is an ancient rumor that this water nurtures greed,
> Moreover, if you drink this water, you will want more than you need.
> I say, my friends that an honest man could not be corrupted so,
> Even if he drank so much water that the well could no longer go.

Wu went on to serve in his prestigious position as a senior officer for many years despite having drunk from the "greedy water." In fact, Wu was able to both maintain and even enhance his reputation as an honest man.

Moral: Greedy water does not corrupt officials. Officials who are corrupt choose to be this way of their own free will.

78. The Country of Madmen

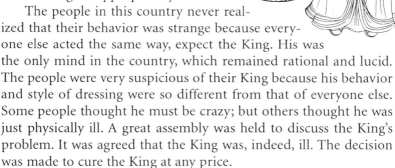

Once upon a time, there was a country full of madmen; they became that way by drinking water out of a "mad spring." Everyone who drank from its water became insane. They would wear fur in the hot summer or a light shirt in the cold winter. They would wear boots on their heads, and hats on their feet. They would argue that black was white and that right was wrong. They might suddenly burst into tears or laugh inappropriately.

The people in this country never realized that their behavior was strange because everyone else acted the same way, expect the King. His was the only mind in the country, which remained rational and lucid. The people were very suspicious of their King because his behavior and style of dressing were so different from that of everyone else. Some people thought he must be crazy; but others thought he was just physically ill. A great assembly was held to discuss the King's problem. It was agreed that the King was, indeed, ill. The decision was made to cure the King at any price.

One day the country people, who were armed with clubs and weapons, attacked and captured the palace. They carried in a barrel of the crazy water and forced the King to drink. When he refused and attempted to escape, the people seized the King and forced his mouth towards the barrel of crazy water, but he still refused to give up. Enraged, the people were now certain that the King was completely mad.

Eventually, the King was taken to the ground, and a cup of crazy water was poured down his throat. Suddenly, the King's eyes glazed over and he gazed up at the sky with a peculiar look on his face; it was evident to all men that he too had finally become good.

The madmen were elated for they realized the King was now behaving exactly like them. They left the palace dancing for joy.

Moral: Be vigilant, for madness can be contagious.

79. The Swimmer's Money

Many rivers and creeks tricked through the valley. Often, local residents frolicked and swam in the streams and pools of this lush river valley. One day the sudden flooding of water running off a nearby mountain abruptly interrupted the residents' carefree water activities.

Six men in a boat were enjoying the relaxed companionship of a leisurely fishing trip on the river, when their boat violently capsized turning them all into the swirling water. Undaunted, the men boldly began to battle high waves, cold winds and rushing currents in an attempt to swim to shore.

One man named Mr. Chu, however, lagged behind the rest of the group. Since Mr. Chu was a superior swimmer, the others were puzzled by his slow return to shore, and called out to him, "Mr. Chu, you are a better swimmer than any one of us, so why are you falling behind the group? Hurry up, or you will drown."

Now much further behind and gasping for breath Mr. Chu shouted, "This morning I tied one thousand copper dollars to my waist—the weight of the money is making it hard for me to swim." From a distance, his friends all began shouting for him to cut the money loose from his waist, or he will be dragged down by the weight of it. Now too weak to speak, Mr. Chu just shook his head refusing to cut loose the money.

Eventually, the other five men exhausted and gasping for breath finally made it to shore. From their place of safety, they were helpless to do anything for Mr. Chu. They observed their friend, now farther away then ever, being swept ceaselessly into ever-stronger currents.

"Mr. Chu," one friend shouted loudly, "You still have a chance to save yourself. Please throw away the money—if you don't, you will most certainly drown."

Mr. Chu, now exhausted, had strength only to shake his head in denial, refusing, to the last, to give up the money.

All that was left to see was the arrival of one last large wave, cresting higher than ever over Mr. Chu, only to swallow him up and his money into its whirling vortex.

Moral: The love of money may cause a man to lose his own life.

80. The Chief Executive Is Besieged

During the Tang Dynasty there was a siege around the city of Ding. Armed brigands so closely besieged Ding that not even a trickle of water could filter into the city.

The Chief Executive of the city was named Sun; he was a weak and incompetent man. Upon hearing that the siege had taken a turn for the worse, Sun ordered that his office be closed. Sun then hid himself in his home with the front and back doors locked and double bolted. Only a small opening in the door would allow a note to be slipped inside.

A few days later the brigand soldiers stormed the city gates and secured Ding for themselves. Sun was so terribly frightened by this turn of events that he threw himself into a closet. Sun then screamed for his house manager to lock the door,

"If any brigands get into this house, whatever you do, do not give them the key to this closet."

Moral: A timid man cannot secure his life by hiding in a closet.

81. The Shadow's Cool Embrace

In ancient times, there was a man who had an abnormal dislike of heat. During summertime, he would often be seen carrying a small mat under his arm. Periodically, he would place the mat under a tree and enjoy the cool shade.

In order to remain in the shadows, as the sun moved the man would move his mat accordingly. At nighttime the man often remained under the tree and enjoyed being completely enveloped by darkness. Eventually the moon rose high in the sky. As the shadow of the moon passed over him, the man moved his mat into the shade as he did with the sun in daylight. Unfortunately, because of the heavy dew, the man's clothes became dreadfully wet and he shivered with cold.

Moral: One may lose one's enjoyment of a favorite place as time changes the situation.

82. The Blind Man and the Sun

Once upon a time, there was a man who was born blind in both eyes. Since this man had never seen the sun, he relied on other people to describe its appearance.

One person described the sun as a copper dish. Someone else said that the sun shines like a candle.

After hearing these two analogies, the blind man decided to buy a candle. After his purchase, he spent time touching and stroking the candle, gradually obtaining an understanding of its shape and texture.

Soon afterwards, the blind man happened upon a short flute. As he touched the flute, he felt it was a similar shape as a candle. Therefore, he came to believe that it was the sun.

Moral: Seeing is believing.

83. A Man Gets Flim-flammed

Once upon a time, there was a naive man named Hu. On impulse, Hu decided to take a journey to a place called Pong Gate. Unprepared for the length of the journey, Hu grew increasingly tired. Mid point from his destination, he was unable to walk another step. As he reached into his pocket, he was delighted to find fifty dollars. Hu decided to hire a boat.

Now the owner of the only available boat was a crafty and cunning individual. He learned that Hu only had fifty dollars and was desperate to hire the boat. Deciding to take advantage of the situation the boat owner said to Hu,

"It is an exceedingly long way you wish to be taken. It is also suspicious that you are alone and have no luggage. For this type of job, I require that you pay me one hundred dollars in advance." Hu, of course, was mortified that he did not have enough money to pay. The boat owner grinned a broad and hypocritical smile and said,

"My friend, money is unimportant to me. Your friendship is what matters. Let me make a deal with you. You are young and therefore have lots of energy. Instead of me rowing, you can walk along the river shore pulling my boat and me forward. As soon as we arrive at your destination of Pong Gate, I'll collect fifty dollars from you—that is, half price."

Delighted at the half price bargain, Hu agreed to the conditions.

Moral: Be vigilant in business affairs. Some unscrupulous individual may trick you into paying for your own services.

84. A Brave Man Learns to Swim

Once upon a time, there was a man renown for his bravery. He lived in the North. In addition to being fearless, he loved athletics and horsemanship. His one weakness was that he did not know how to swim.

The brave man often gazed longingly at swimmers diving gracefully into the water. Observing their moves, he determined that swimming was not that difficult after all.

Determined to achieve the divers' prowess, he asked them to teach him how to swim. The swimmers were happy to describe in detail the proper techniques for floating, swimming and diving. The brave man was an eager and attentive listener. The man determined that the art of swimming was a simple one. Hence he quickly rushed to the river and threw himself into the water.

The man was admittedly surprised to find the water above his head. Gasping for breath, he promptly forgot every instruction he had so recently learned. His panic increasing, his mind could muster only one thought: "HELP."

Finally after many gulps, gasps and bubbles, the man succumbed to the swirling water and was drowned together with all of the verbal instructions about how to swim.

Moral: Three key words for learning a technique are: practice, practice, practice.

85. The Copper Vase

Once upon a time in the city of Luoyang, there lived a quite ordinary man by the name of Shen. One day as Shen was planting some tomato seeds in his garden, he happened to dig up an extraordinarily beautiful copper vase. Turquoise in color, and featuring unicorns grazing beneath serene clouds, Shen guessed that the vase dated back to the Han Dynasty.

Shen had a greedy neighbor by the name of Lu. When Lu saw the beauty of the vase, he coveted one for himself. Lu, therefore, hired a professional craftsman to create an exact copy. After the copy was completed, Lu treated it with a special aging chemical, then buried it in the ground. Three years later, Lu dug up the fake vase. It was now a replica of Shen's original.

One day Lu perceived an opportunity to ingratiate himself with a local nobleman. He presented the nobleman with the vase. The nobleman, believing that Lu had gifted him with a genuine treasure, organized an elaborate banquet in his honor. The imposter vase was mounted in the center of the table for all the nobleman's friends and relatives to praise.

As fate would have it, Shen was also invited to this banquet. When he observed the imposter vase, Shen's face drained of its color, then it turned quite red. Standing up, Shen announced in a shaky voice,

"I am sorry to have to tell you this, but your vase is a fake. I have one exactly like it and mine is the real one."

It was now the nobleman's turn to grow red in the face. He too stood up and demanded that Shen go home and then return with his vase.

Some time later, Shen returned with his vase. Now the two vases were placed together like twins in the center of the table: there was no telling them apart.

The nobleman turned to his now captive and quite fascinated audience and announced,

"Obviously my vase is the original and yours is the fake one. You are both a liar and a troublemaker."

The guests, knowing which side of the bread their butter lay on, agreed wholeheartedly with the nobleman.

Shen did his best to argue the point but the nobleman's people had already pre-determined in their minds whom to support. He never stood a chance.

Shen left the banquet with a heavy heart. Shivering with anger at their accusation and at the injustice of it all, he came to understand that it was better to be an ordinary and honest man than to be an abusive snob.

Moral: *Those who abuse their power bend the truth so that black appears white and a deer becomes a horse.*

86. The Blind Man on the Bridge

Once upon a time, there was a blind man who was walking alone across an old bridge. Years ago, the blind man recalled, a deep creek ran beneath this bridge. Since that time, however, the water had dried up and people now bypassed the bridge and simply walked across the dry creek. The blind man, though, had no way of knowing this.

When he was about in the middle of the dilapidated bridge, he stepped on a particularly rotten piece of wood and his feet gave way. Snatching wildly at the anything to secure himself, he grabbed the fence railing with his right hand. Fortunately, his fall was arrested. Hanging from one hand, his feet dangling dangerously, the blind man was terrified of falling into the rushing water below.

"Help me," he screamed loudly, "I'm blind and am going to drown."

His cries alerted a man who was walking his dog nearby. Rushing up to the bridge the man immediately assessed the situation.

"Sir. Don't be afraid. There is no water underneath you. If you just let go, it is less than a three foot drop to completely dry ground."

The blind man neither believed nor trusted the passerby. "I know why you want me to let go: so you can watch me fall into the water and have a good laugh at my expense. Thanks. I'm not that stupid."

Stubbornly he clung onto the fence railing and continued to cry out for help. Eventually the passerby shrugged his shoulders and wandered away with his dog.

The blind man continued to scream for help until his voice became hoarse. Exhausted he could no longer hold on. With his free hand he squeezed his nose and held his breath then jumped. Wham.

A second later he found himself standing on dry solid ground. His first thought was one of immense relief. He was safe and on solid ground. His second thought was for the throbbing ache making its way from his right pinkie finger all the way up his arm and into his neck. Now he was in genuine pain and feeling foolish for not believing the passerby,

"If I had only trusted him," he thought ruefully, "I would not have hung there for such a long time and would not have what is now developing into a first class migraine headache."

Moral: *Sometimes we need to trust the benevolent advice of strangers.*

87. The Discriminating Monk

During the time of the Song Dynasty there was a junior officer named Qiu. One day Qiu, who walked with a cane, traveled to a Buddhist temple on the outskirts of the city. When he arrived, he asked for an audience with a certain monk named Shen.

Now Shen was a particularly haughty monk, always putting on airs, exceedingly conscious of a person's social position. Upon hearing that Qiu was only a minor court official, Shen decided that he was not worth wasting his time on.

The monk kept Qiu waiting an inordinately long time in a drafty hallway. Finally, he was ushered into a small inner room. The monk neither bothered to stand up nor offer Qiu a chair, let alone any kind of refreshment. Barely acknowledging Qiu's presence, he kept his eyes on the papers before him and bluntly stated that he could afford no longer than five minutes of his time.

In spite of the monk's rudeness, Qiu began to state his business. He could barely get two words out before another monk entered the room and informed Shen that the son of a general was here to see him.

Shen leapt up and left the room in a great hurry not even bothering to say one word to Qiu. From this inner room, Qiu observed the way in which the monk treated his honorable guest. Bowing and smiling incessantly, the monk ushered the general's son into an elaborate hall where he was immediately invited to sit in a deep and comfortable chair. Next, the monk ordered that the table be set with the best goblets and chopsticks. He even pleaded with the general's son to stay for supper, saying,

"Excellency, I would consider it the greatest honor if you would taste some special treats and delicacies reserved only for someone as important as yourself."

In spite of Shen's pleas and kowtowing, the general's son refused any refreshment and, concluding his business in some haste, departed quickly.

Leaning against his cane, his throat now quite parched with thirst, Qiu boiled with anger. Outwardly, however, he retained his composure.

When the monk returned to the small room Qiu confronted

him directly,

"A Buddhist monk is supposed to treat all people with respect and dignity. I was made to feel like some insignificant low-life while you practically fell over yourself in an attempt to ingratiate yourself to the general's son. Why is that?"

The monk seemed surprised by the official's question. Feeling no shame or remorse, however, the monk responded in a crafty manner,

"You have completely misunderstood my motives. You do not understand my heart. Everyone to whom I show respect I really dislike, and everyone I disrespect, I really like. In short, to respect is not to respect and to like is not to like."

At these convoluted words, Qiu's anger grew into righteous wrath. Lifting his cane up high, the official let fly several decisive blows upon the monk's addled brain. Cringing in a cowardly manner, the monk cried,

"Why did you do that?"

Qiu, now calm and controlled replied with a smile,

"My old master of Buddhism told me that I needed to understand his mind. It works thus: to beat someone apparently means not to have beaten him; and to not beat someone means he has already been beaten."

Moral: Treat someone as you would like yourself to be treated.

88. The Clean Son-in-law

There was once a famous calligrapher from the Song Dynasty by the name of Mi. Scrupulously clean in all his habits; his fixation with neatness made him an obsessive-compulsive personality.

When Mi's daughter had reached a marriageable age, he began to search for a suitable son-in-law. Since Mi was both famous and wealthy, his daughter was considered quite a catch.

Eligible young bachelors beat a hasty path to Mi's door, only to find a long line of like-minded and ambitious men there before them. Some of these young men were recommended by matchmakers, others came of their own volition. Mi did not care how they came or why, he was interested in only one thing: was the potential candidate clean enough?

Hundreds of candidates applied for the position of son-in-law, but none passed the relentless questions put forth by the meticulous interviewer Mi. They were simply not clean enough.

One day a young scholar from Nanjing, the Southern capital, came to hear about Mi's unusual requirements for a son-in-law. Perceiving an opportunity for an easy life, he decided to apply for the position. Mi took note of his clean appearance, admiring his fine white skin and neatly pressed clothes. As usual, Mi began by asking the bachelor his name and place of birth.

"My surname is 'Tidiness' and my given name is 'Dust-free.' I was born in the Southern capital in a district called 'sanitary,' in the borough of 'Health.' My nick-name is 'Unsoiled.'"

Mi was overjoyed to hear all of this information and, equating such names as 'Tidiness' with a character trait, he agreed to the match on the spot. Soon Mi had a new son-in-law of whom he was exceedingly giddy with pride.

Mi did not know, however, what his daughter came to learn after the marriage. Her new husband was the quintessential slob. Both messy and dirty, he was the most slovenly individual to ever come within her field of reference. When she had the occasion to visit his old home, she was astonished to see that entire colonies of spiders had been allowed to nest unmolested for years. Further, he had never taken a bath his whole life except once when he fell into a river by mistake. She was stuck with him.

Moral: A person's name does not necessarily reflect his character.

89. Portrait of an Ugly Man

Once upon a time, there lived a man who was very ugly indeed. He commissioned an artist to draw a portrait of himself. When the portrait was completed, the man viewed it with disdain. Convinced that he did not look like that, he ordered the artist to re-do the portrait.

Upon viewing the second attempt, the man was still disappointed. He believed that he looked a lot better than the artist had portrayed him. Refusing to pay until the portrait looked the way the man believed himself to be, the artist drew it over and over again many times. After the fifth attempt, the man accused the artist of deliberately making him appear worse than he actually looked.

The artist's patience finally came to the end. Now thoroughly provoked, he leaned towards the man and, thrusting his pointer finger in his face, said,

"I have attempted to make you appear better in the drawing than you actually look. Instead of thanking me, you blame me because you are ugly. If I were now to draw you as you actually are, people would be afraid to look at it."

Moral: It is important to have a truthful self-image.

90. The Mistaken Eulogy

Once upon a time, there was a wealthy man who decided to hold a memorial service for his mother-in-law. His father-in-law was particularly touched by the gesture.

This wealthy man had an illiterate relative who had been very fond of the deceased. The illiterate man was determined, therefore, to read the eulogy at the memorial service. He got the services of a retired school teacher to write an appropriate eulogy. This teacher was quite elderly and shortsighted. He spent much time searching for the perfect eulogy. In so doing, he searched through many antique manuscripts. Though he always grew dizzy from heights, he nonetheless braved wobbly ladders in the library. Giddy from the swaying heights and a victim of poor vision anyway, he finally located the perfect eulogy: beautiful words from an antique text specially designed as a memorial for a father-in-law. After painstakingly writing down the beautiful words, the teacher presented the parchment to the illiterate man. On the day of the memorial service, the man pinned the parchment to a wall in a prominent location. Everyone who attended the service read it including his father-in-law.

Finally, the wealthy man, responding to many complaints, had occasion to read the parchment himself. His face now burned red with indignation. Tearing it from the wall, he then had his illiterate relative forcefully ejected from the building.

Now the illiterate man was in an exceedingly bad humor. He had no idea why the family had rejected his eulogy and treated him so badly. Stewing with frustration, he decided that the teacher must have played a hoax on him.

He confronted the teacher and demanded an explanation.

Now the teacher got his back up and refused any kind of criticism, saying,

"I wrote the eulogy word for word from a classic text. It was proofread and edited with the greatest amount of care. I guarantee that there was not a single mistake in it. As I see it, your family made the mistake. The person who died made the error of dying while the person who is alive has made the error of living."

Moral: Illiterate people suffer many misfortunes.

91. The Light from the Firefly and the Snow

Once upon a time, there were two poor and threadbare scholars. They spent all their time and what little money they had on books. One was called Che Yin, the other Sun Kang. In order to conserve the costly oil lamp for night reading they each found ingenious methods for reading in the dim winter daylight.

Che caught a brightly-lit firefly and housed it in a transparent cheesecloth bag. He was able to read quite well from the firefly's bright light.

Sun moved his books outside. He carefully positioned his books on a table beside the snow: the glare reflected from the sun onto the snow created a perfect reading lamp.

Through their two unique and frugal methods for light, both Che and Sun became famous. Now they were both wealthy and could afford to indulge in their passion for reading.

Celebrity and affluence, however, had the effect of making Che and Sun competitive.

One day Sun went to Che's home to pay him a visit. Che's servant informed Sun that his master was out looking for a larger, more efficient firefly. Hearing these words, Sun left quickly, and determined, himself, to improve his snow reading method.

A few days later Che went to pay Sun a visit. The moon shone brightly as he arrived at Sun's home at midnight. Che found Sun sitting outside without any books staring up into the sky.

Perplexed, Che asked him,

"The moon is shining so brightly tonight. Why don't you take advantage of this bright light to read?"

Sun frowned sadly and said,

"From the look of the sky there won't be any snow tonight."

Moral: The purpose of reading is to learn other perspectives and expand your vision. Knowledge without wisdom, however, is useless.

92. A Pot of Boiling Fish

Once upon a time, seven blind men lived together in the mountain area. These men had never eaten fish. One day they decided that they would all like to taste fish for the first time. They could only afford to purchase enough fresh fish to feed four men. In order to spread the meal around they decided to make fish soup.

As the water in the soup pot reached its boil, the fish were dropped inside. The fish, greatly disliking the temperature of the water, flipped themselves out of the pot one by one. The blind men, however, were completely ignorant of this occurrence. Eventually the blind men perceived that the fish soup was done. Dancing with joy, they convinced themselves that this was going to be the best meal they had ever eaten. They even decided to save all their money to buy fresh fish.

As the blind men sat before their bowls ready to partake of the fish soup, a small fish suddenly flopped onto the hand of one man.

"Wait," he shouted to the others. "Do not eat. The fish are not in the pot; they are alive and flipping around. Find them, quickly."

All seven men bent down on their hands and knees and felt around the ground for the elusive fish. Eventually all the fish were retrieved and placed back into the pot.

Initially they felt regret by this unfortunate turn of events. Eventually, however, their good humor was restored and they were all happy again.

One man spoke for the group when he said,

"It's actually a good thing that the fish jumped out of the pot. They were too fresh and might have killed us. They were too good to be eaten. Now, they are more seasoned and better to eat."

Moral: Forget the past and move forward.

93. The Two Stupid Sons

Once upon a time, there was an extremely wealthy man whose assets were estimated to be over ten million dollars. This rich man lived a life of luxury with his two sons. Now both of this rich man's sons were stupid but one was more stupid than the other. The rich man so loved his sons that he was entirely blinded to their stupidity. In fact, he had convinced himself that because they were handsome and dressed well that they were both bright and intelligent. Because the man was so rich and powerful, no one had ever set him straight on the matter.

One day a friend, equally wealthy and powerful, came from a far away place for a visit. After a few days of observing his friend's sons, the man decided that it was time for some straight talk.

"My friend, please do not take offense with what I am about to say, for I am only telling you what everyone else is afraid to. Your two sons are quite handsome and they dress well. However, I am concerned about what will happen when you grow old. Those two sons of yours are so scatter-brained that they will never be able to run the affairs of your estate."

Now the rich man did not take this information well. Deeply insulted, he said,

"How dare you cast aspersions on my sons. If what you say is true, why have I never heard it before? Your problem is that you are jealous I have two such fine sons."

The rich man's friend spread his hands in a reconciliatory gesture,

"Please do not take offense. My only motive for telling you is friendship. Indeed, if you think carefully about it, the matter can be resolved with a simple test. After all, a good horse does not fear a race."

Still upset, but determined to prove his friend wrong, the rich man replied,

"I agree. My sons can pass any test you can think of."

His friend replied,

"Then I propose you ask them where rice comes from."

Now the rich man was extremely angry; to ask such an easy question that an infant could answer was insulting. However, determined to prove his friend wrong and get this unpleasant business behind him, he agreed to the question. His two sons were subsequently summoned into the room.

"Where does rice come from?" the father asked his elder son.

Puffing out his chest and grinning idiotically, the elder replied, "Everybody knows that. Rice comes from the kitchen."

Now the rich man blushed an extraordinary shade of crimson. Turning to his younger son, he repeated the question with tight lips, "Where does rice come from?"

The younger son, who was even more stupid and boastful than his elder brother, completely missed his father's extremely obvious anger. He winked with one eye, then with the other before replying, "That's an easy one. Rice comes from the rice bag."

Now the father's blush turned an even deeper shade of red. His lips were pinched together in anger as he addressed his sons directly,

"Idiots. You have made a complete fool out of me. What have you been doing all these years instead of learning—fooling around no doubt? For your information, rice does not come from the kitchen or from a bag. It comes from our rice warehouse."

Moral: You should not try to bluff your way through something you know nothing about. Such pretense is evident to all who witness it.

94. The Dismantled Bell

In ancient times, two main government officials ruled the Qi State. These were the senior officers of the Premier and the Vice-Premier.

One day the King of Qi decided that the state capital should be moved to a different city. The officers of the Premier and Vice-Premier worked together to ensure that the transition was an orderly one. The workers, however, were unable to find a way to dislodge and move the heavy bell from the bell tower. This particular bell weighed five thousand pounds. Experts estimated that five hundred strong-backed men were needed to move it.

There were very few strong men remaining in the capital; most of the young men had been recruited to the front as guards. The laborers who were available numbered less than fifty. This problem was first reported to the Vice-Premier. Unable to come up with a solution, he referred the matter to the Premier's office.

When his re-location officer reported the dilemma to him, the Premier leaned far back in his chair, pursed his lips together and stared upwards. Lifting his hand to his face, he absently twisted his finger around the hairs of his beard. Finally, he sat up straight and regarded his re-location officer disdainfully,

"I can not believe the kind of trivial matters you decide to bring before me. What is wrong with you? The solution is so simple that a child could figure it out. The bell weighs five thousand pounds, so you think that five hundred men are required to move about ten pounds each. That reasoning is ridiculous. Here is what you do: chisel the bell into five hundred pieces. Then hire one person to carry each piece five hundred times. It's that simple."

The re-location officer was amazed by the Premier's brilliant solution, and hurried away to carry out the orders.

When the Vice-Premier learned of his superior's solution, he sighed deeply,

"Our Premier is a person of unique talent. However, after the bell is moved in that manner it will end up as a waste pile of iron."

Moral: The end does not justify the means.

95. The Prime Minister's Calligraphy

At one time during the Song Dynasty there was a Prime Minister named Zhang. At best, his calligraphy could be described as average. However, he thought of himself as something of an expert in both calligraphy and the composition of poetry.

One morning, feeling particularly prosaic, he wrote out some verses with an elaborate flourish. Unfortunately, the characters were entirely illegible. He then gave the verses to his nephew to copy out in regular script.

His nephew gazed at the unseemly characters with great incomprehension. As he studied the convoluted lines, they began to look less like words and more like an attempt at pre-abstract art.

Eventually the nephew gave up and returned the script to his uncle. With a shameful look, the boy said,

"Uncle, I am very sorry to say that I can not read your writing. Could you please tell me what it says?"

With an exasperated sigh, the Prime Minister accepted the script and peered intently at it.

A confused look came over his face. He wrinkled his brows and studied the characters carefully. He tried to read the words from left to right and from right to left. The more he tried to understand his writing, the less it made sense.

Crumpling the paper up with rage, the Prime Minister threw it at his nephew.

"Idiot," he barked. "Why didn't you bring this to me right away when the words were fresh in my mind? Now my brilliant composition is lost forever."

Moral: If the handwriting is illegible, what use is the content to the reader?

96. The Priceless Zither

One day a craftsman named Wang obtained some top quality wood from the paulownia tree. With this wood, he fashioned a zither. Wang crafted the many strings of the instrument to perfection. When completed the music from his creation sounded melodious and sweet, like gold and jade vibrating together in harmony. Wang was very pleased with his accomplishment.

In fact, the instrument was so superior in sound that musicians were hard-pressed to find another with which to compare.

Wang, a benevolent music-lover himself, decided to donate his special instrument to the Court of Music. Upon presentation to the court, he humbly explained that the zither had the finest pitch of any instrument in the country. Zither players from around the country came to see if Wang's claim were true.

Wang was astonished by their assessment. The expert zither players took one look and disdained to even touch the instrument. They were unanimous in their assessment that the instrument was too new to be any good. This zither, he was informed, was not worth even one unit of gold. The Court of Music officials then returned the zither back to Wang.

On his way home, Wang stewed with rage. The zither players had refused to even try out the instrument. The assessment was based on its age not its musical quality. Determined to make the experts eat their words, Wang conceived an idea.

When he was home, he hired the services of a lacquer expert. According to Wang's instructions, the expert set about "aging" the instrument. Several scratches and broken lines now scarred the surface. Some characters were removed from the side. Then the zither was placed in a wooden box and buried in the ground to age.

One year later Wang dug up the zither. It was stained with earth and some rot had set into the side. Now the decayed zither was ready to take to the market place. Determined to press home his point, Wang charged a thoroughly ridiculous price.

A wealthy nobleman happened to be in the market place. When he spotted the zither, his eyes widened in disbelief. Believing he had found a buried treasure, he gladly paid the one hundred units of gold and purchased the instrument on the spot.

The nobleman carefully wrapped the zither in costly yellow silk, then presented it to the King as a special gift. The King summoned all the music experts to his court to determine the zither's value.

The same musicians who had just one year ago assessed Wang's zither so disparagingly now had only praise for it. The most senior of the musicians assessed it as follows:

"I have lived seventy years in the world and have seen thousands of zithers. Not until this moment have I witnessed such absolute perfection. It is like a huge flawless diamond unearthed in all its glory. Its color, style, and fragrance also speak of its history. It is a priceless antique beyond compare."

Moral: The key word in music appraisal is music.

97. The Rich Monk and the Poor Monk

Once upon a time, there were two monks who lived in a boarder town of the Sichuan Province. One monk was rich and the other monk was poor. One day the poor monk addressed the rich monk,

"For some time now I have longed to make a pilgrimage to the top of the mountain by the East Sea. I have decided that the time is right to make the journey. Would you like to accompany me?"

The rich monk shook his head and said disdainfully,

"You are completely unrealistic. It is thousands of miles to the East Sea. The way is blocked by a mountain range and wide rivers. Further, there are many other natural barriers. If all of that is not enough, you don't have a penny to your name. How could you possibly make it?"

The poor monk humbly replied,

"My pilgrimage will be a journey of faith. I will travel by foot. I will carry a bottle of water and an alms bowl for food. I will rely on the kindness of strangers to feed and house me."

The rich monk was surprised by these words and objected further,

"Look, for years, I myself have longed to go on such a pilgrimage. Eventually I will buy a boat and travel by sea. It is simply unrealistic of you to think that you can make the journey alone and on foot."

One year later the poor monk returned from his pilgrimage to the top of the mountain by the East Sea. All had gone well and his goal had been accomplished.

Now the rich monk felt ashamed.

Moral: Where there is a will, there is a way.

98. The Keen Designer

During the Song Dynasty there was a Prime Minister named Wang Anshi. This man was a great political reformer who made major changes for the better during his time in office.

During the time of Wang's tenure, it soon became known among those in political circles that to be promoted one had to adopt a policy of political reform. This knowledge was the cause for much competition among ambitious politicos.

One local designer in particular was desperately keen to be promoted ahead of the others. In order to achieve recognition the designer hastily crafted together a plan for population control. Posturing with flamboyance, he informed the Prime Minister of his brilliant idea, "The previous administration, known for having kept the status quo, was unwilling to come up with a solution for population control. I, however, have found the ideal solution for our new policies of reform."

The Prime Minister became excited by the prospect of a solution to this seemingly unsolvable problem. Together with his Vice-Premier, they encouraged the designer to continue. Smiling broadly, his chest puffed out to its fullest, the designer said, "The main problem is the lack of farmland to accommodate all the people. Further, because of the lack of arable land, the grain harvest is severely limited—this has had adverse economic effects. I propose that we dry the lake surrounding the Liang Mountain. Potentially, this would provide six or eight hundred new square miles of prime land for rice paddies. The yield from such a harvest would increase by tens of thousands of pounds annually."

The Prime Minister was very excited by the proposition. He smiled broadly and shook his head up and down as he counted all the profits in his head. Suddenly, his smile left him and his eyebrows drew together. In a puzzled voice, he asked the designer, "Where is the water in the eight hundred square miles of lake going to go?"

At these words, the designer also lost his smile. His eyes widened and his chin fell to his chest. He and the Prime Minister continued to stare at each other.

Finally, the Vice-Premier, quick-witted and never one to miss the humor in such absurdity, offered, "The difficulty is easily overcome. Just dig out an eight hundred square mile pond beside the lake and put all the water in it."

Moral: Think before you speak.

99. The Harmony Brothers

Once upon a time, there were three brothers who all lived together in the same household with their wives and children. Though the wives and children all got along, the three brothers argued constantly, each disputing the other in just about everything.

One day the eldest brother addressed his younger brothers,

"Look, our parents have passed away. We have been left this family home to share. We are blood. We should not be arguing like we do over every little thing. Can you just imagine our parents looking down at us from heaven in shame?"

The two younger brothers agreed with the eldest. Now they all felt ashamed about their petty quarreling, and promised each other to change for the better. Then the eldest brother put forth a proposition.

"Since we all agree that we are going to change our ways, let us make sure we remain in harmony. If anyone creates a problem or a quarrel then a fine will be imposed on him. He must pay for dinner for the entire household."

The brothers all agreed that this was an excellent solution to ensure harmony. Determined to change their ways, they all vowed to avoid arguments of any kind or pay for dinner for the entire household. Satisfied, they all went to their separate rooms for the night.

The next morning the three brothers were assembled at the breakfast table. The eldest brother opened up a topic for discussion,

"Did you hear what happened last night? Someone stole the well from the east side of our street and moved it over to the west side."

The second brother was just about to say, "I don't believe it," when he stopped himself. Remembering their vow not to argue, he carefully re-phrased his words,

"I do believe it. In fact, I even heard a sound in the night like rushing water. At first, I thought it must be a flood. Then I heard someone mention something about a stolen well."

The third brother, however, just blurted out the first thing that came to his mind,

"Ridiculous. How could a well be stolen? You made up that entire story."

With a stern expression on his face, the eldest brother said,

"You have started an argument and broken your vow. Now, you must pay for dinner."

The third brother had no choice. He retreated to his room for a sulk. There, he told his wife the entire story. Now his wife was a very astute and intelligent woman. Taking the money from her husband's hand, she promised to fix things. Standing before her brothers-in-law, she addressed them thus,

"My dearest brothers-in-law. Let me tell you what just now happened to your younger brother. He complained about a pain in his stomach. I assumed that he had a touch of the flu. Imagine my surprise when he gave birth to a baby. Oh well. Here is the money he asked me to deliver to you."

The eldest brother wrinkled up his face in derision, then said,

"What is this nonsense? I don't believe for one second that a man can have a baby, let alone my idiot brother."

His sister-in-law then replied sweetly,

"This time, it is you who broke your vow. I will not ask you to pay me, but neither will I pay you."

Moral: Real harmony takes work and stems from familial love and respect.

100. The Counterfeit Wine

There was once a time, long ago, when the Shandong people did not know how to ferment wine well. Only the Zhongshan people knew how to ferment wine, and they did it well. It became known far and wide as the best wine money could buy. The Zhongshan people held a monopoly on the wine trade and, determined to keep it that way, refused to share their secret with anyone.

Now the Shandong people were equally determined to acquire the recipe.

A crafty Shandong businessman traveled to Zhongshan on the pretence of discussing trade relations with the government. Once there, he was invited to a party at the distillery owned by a wine exporter. When no one was looking, the crafty man seized the opportunity to steal some of the brewer's mash used to ferment the wine.

Returning home to Shandong, the businessman promptly opened up a wine shop. He simply soaked the awful tasting local wine in with the stolen brewer's mash. He then promoted the wine far and wide claiming that it was made from the Zhongshan's original secret recipe.

At the grand opening, only nobles and high ranking government officials and wealthy citizens were invited to taste the wine. The reception to this new treat was staggering. The Governor of the State said,

"Many years ago when I was in Zhongshan, I had the pleasure of tasting their unforgettable wine. I am happy to say that this wine tastes exactly like the original."

Everyone was exceedingly happy that Zhongshan no longer had a monopoly on this most excellent tasting wine. They proclaimed the businessman a genius. Elaborate plans were made for expansion and exportation.

Meanwhile, months went by and the wine shop flourished. It was always full of customers eager to purchase this exceptional wine that was the talk of the town.

Finally, the rumors surrounding the new Shandong wine reached the ears of the wine brewers in Zhongshan. The chief wine brewer decided to pay the crafty Shandong businessman a visit.

When the chief wine brewer tasted the Shandong wine, his eyes watered and he immediately spat it out.

"Yuck," he said in disgust. Then his face broke out into a broad smile,

"You know, I really worried about all the stories I heard that you had imitated our exceptional wine. I'm so glad I came all the way here for a taste. Now I know the truth. Your wine is nothing more than our brewer's mash mixed with bad wine. It's the worst tasting stuff I've ever had in my life."

His smile grew even bigger and he said,

"I'm so relieved."

Moral: To discern quality one needs to have a discriminating taste.

101. Ladies Five, Eight, and Nine

Once upon a time, there was a lady named Five who married a County Governor. In support of her husband, Lady Five always accompanied him to high society social functions.

One day, the Governor and Lady Five attended a wedding at the home of one of the wealthiest families in the county. At the wedding banquet they were introduced to important guests, including the County Administrator and the County Secretary, who were accompanied by their respective wives.

During the banquet, Lady Five, whose husband's rank was above that of all the other guests, asked the Administrator's wife her name. The reply was, "My name is Six."

Startled, Lady Five inquired after the name of the Secretary's wife, who replied, "My name is Seven."

Upon hearing these names, Lady Five became angry. She threw down her chopsticks, stood up, turned, and flounced out of the room in a huff. The other wives, confused and upset by the behavior of Lady Five, wanted to leave themselves.

The host of the banquet, observing the commotion, approached Lady Five as she departed. When he inquired about the source of her grief, she replied,

"As the governor's wife, I thought it my duty to learn the names of the other important guests and their wives. To my surprise, however, I learned that one wife is named Six and the other is Seven. I think that the two wives were deliberately named thus because, just as their names are superior to mine numerically, it would imply that they are superior socially. I find this lack of protocol insulting. Furthermore, I'm sure that if I asked two more ladies their names, they would be Eight and Nine."

Moral: A person can change his or her name, but it doesn't change who he or she is.

Reader's Notes

Reader's Notes

Reader's Notes